Infatuations

Barbara Winkes

ISBN: 978-1-0693045-3-7

Cover art © May Dawney Designs

Created with Atticus

For D.

Chapter One

I f she spent much more time on doing her hair, she'd be late. The last thing Ellie wanted on the first day of her new job was to be late. She already knew the people she'd work with, which was both a blessing and a challenge. There'd be expectations, though it was unclear whether they'd be more demanding than the ones she had for herself.

With a sigh, she took out all the pins and combed out her hair, deciding that a ponytail would work. She'd been wearing her hair in a bun at work on most days, since day one—it was time for something different.

After a knock on the door, Jordan leaned against the doorframe. Ellie could see her smile in the mirror.

"What?"

"You're going to wear that?"

"Why not? If you don't like it, I'm sorry. I don't have time to change again."

"I like it all right, but you want to be in those shoes all day?"

Ellie looked down to her feet and shrugged. The heels were a moderate height.

"They're not that high. I'll be fine. Don't get me wrong. I was proud wearing the uniform, but this is me too. This is what I always wanted."

"I know. And you got it. Congratulations." Jordan walked over to her and kissed her, then she turned to the mirror as well. "Hm. I feel a bit underdressed. Maybe *I* should change."

"No," they said at the same time, laughing.

"Come on, let's go. You don't want to be late on the first day."

"Tell me about it," Ellie mumbled, finally acknowledging the butterflies in her stomach. She had worked towards this day her whole career. She was ready.

She was nervous.

"You'll be fine," Jordan said, her hand on Ellie's shoulder a gentle reminder that they needed to go.

"Yes, I will be."

Eventually.

"Do we have another D.A.? Oh, it's Harding. I almost didn't recognize you."

Ellie just smiled. She wasn't too surprised at the occasional stare, or Waters' joke referring to her clothes. She knew she was well within the department's regulations. Jordan's partner Derek Henderson wore a suit almost every day while Jordan and Maria Doss favored more casual wear.

"Well, it's a good thing you look the same. Since we're going to work together."

"Yeah, I guess the lieutenant thought I could show you the ropes before I leave. Listen carefully—you might learn something."

Waters wasn't the most liked colleague in the unit, but Ellie didn't mind. She would listen and learn indeed and ignore the rest. He was going to retire in a few months. Her career as a detective was just beginning. She wasn't going to let him deter her in any way. She had worked with the detectives on multiple occasions and was far from the complete newbie he made her out to be. So far, so good.

"Ellie, good morning. Have a good first day. Cliff."

Maria Doss, Waters' old partner, was whistling to herself as she walked past them, obviously content to be working solo for the foreseeable future.

Listen and learn, Ellie reminded herself when Lieutenant Carroll opened the door of his office.

"Waters, Harding, come in here for a minute."

Ellie hurried to keep up with the senior detective, self-consciously aware of the sound her heels made on the floor. Perhaps Jordan did have a point earlier, but she'd have to work hard to make Ellie admit it. She barely suppressed a smile. She had the job she always wanted, and a beautiful home she shared with the woman she loved, and she was going to marry.

Could life be any better?

The lieutenant's brief, matter-of-fact delivery brought Ellie's enthusiasm down a few notches.

"A homeless person was found dead in Patton Lake Park. A jogger called it in. There are unis on the scene."

"Another one?" Ellie frowned. "There was a man said to have died from exposure last month, in the same area." A few weeks ago, the temperature had been in the tens, unusually low for the season. It was possible.

"If the ME said he died from exposure, you are probably safe to assume that," Waters said.

"If this is not a homicide, then it seems like the city has another problem altogether." Lieutenant Carroll looked decidedly unhappy. "All right, get me some answers. And Harding, welcome."

"Thank you, Lieutenant."

It was a beautiful day, the sun high and bright as they drove out to Patton Lake Park in Waters' Crown Vic. Yet, a person's life had ended, possibly, in the course of a criminal act. That person might have been a mother, a sister, or a friend to someone. Ellie had assisted in investigations, taped off crime scenes, canvassed neighborhoods for witnesses—this time, finding justice for the victim was her responsibility. She would do everything she could to achieve that goal, and make the people who mattered in her life, proud.

Truth be told, Ellie had considered even higher heels, as everyone had teased her about how she'd likely spend her first week—at least—doing her senior partner's paperwork. When they exited the car and walked along the winding path near the lake, she was glad she'd opted for a more sensible choice. It wasn't hard to find the right place—a crowd of curious onlookers had already gathered. Closer to the scene, a young, uniformed cop was doing her best to keep them at bay.

"Please, step back." She drew a sharp breath before tying the end of the yellow tape to a tree.

Ellie thought she looked painfully young. That would have been her, only a few years ago. Waters ducked under the tape, and she hurried over to him.

"Sir, you can't..." She blushed when she realized who he was.

"Detectives Waters and Harding, if this one can make it all the way without ruining her shoes," he said dryly.

Ellie kept quiet, unwilling to argue over something so mundane. She hadn't complained, and her shoes would be fine. The grass was still slightly wet from last night's rain, which didn't bode well for finding clues as to how the woman had died.

"Hey. Meet Officer Potts from the new batch of rookies." Ellie was glad to see a familiar face in Casey Lyons.

"She's twelve," she whispered. "Did I ever look this young?"

Casey laughed. "'We all did at some point. Of course, you are all grown up now."

"What do you have?" Ellie asked before she'd invite any more comments on her wardrobe.

"Over here."

She and Waters followed Casey a little further down the slight slope where the body had been dumped near a cluster of bushes. The medical examiner, Dr. Adams, was crouching next to the dead woman.

"Dana Jacobs jogs here every morning. She said she wouldn't have noticed anything, but she stopped to catch her breath, and she realized what she mistook for a bag of clothes, was in fact a dead person."

Ellie got her first look at the body and winced. The woman's age was hard to gauge, but she seemed to be in her fifties or sixties. Long stringy hair was sticking to her face. The rain had washed away most of the blood, but some had soaked into her clothes, still visible. She leaned closer, her stomach lurching at the sight of the head wound.

"Harding!" Waters said sharply.

"It's okay. I'm fine." "Fine" might have been the understatement of the year, but Ellie was certain she wasn't going to throw up. "I guess it's fair to say exposure didn't do that to her," she said.

"No kidding." Dr. Adams looked up at her. "See this?" She pointed to a hole in the dead woman's sweater. "That's where the blade went in. Of course, there's this..."

It wasn't until now that Ellie realized she was seeing small fragments of skull. She hoped her promise wasn't premature. No. Not on the first day. She had faced some gruesome sights in her time as a uniformed officer. She had to keep it together.

"Can you say which came first?"

Melissa Adams shrugged. "I'll know after the autopsy, but I'm pretty sure either one would be enough. Looks like overkill to me."

"Yeah...Maybe he was toying with her."

"Wild guesses aren't really helpful," Waters reminded her of his presence. "I'll go talk to Ms. Jacobs."

"Okay." Ellie straightened and took a look around. Patton Lake was a popular destination for locals and tourists. In the distance, she could see a playground with swings and a sandbox. Again, the rain proved to be a disadvantage—if Jane Doe had been killed last night, it was unlikely that many people had been out. She shielded her eyes from the sun to look at the bystanders. A group of teenagers with phones, various people of all ages who seemed to have just walked by and found nothing better to do than gawk at a place where a person had died—or at least, found dead.

Her eyes met those of a young man who lacked the sensationalist enthusiasm of the others. He wore a shabby coat tied tightly, a plastic bag in his hand, his expression solemn.

"Excuse me," Ellie said to Dr. Adams, then walked briskly towards the man. When he saw her coming in his direction, he turned on his heels and started to run.

"Police! Stop! I just want to talk to you!" Just her luck that the first day was everything but boring paperwork. He didn't listen. She followed him all the way up to a fence, where he climbed right over.

Ellie cursed, but a moment later, Officer Potts arrived from the other side. The man realized he had nowhere to go and let himself be cuffed.

"Thanks, Potts. Great job."

"You're welcome."

"I didn't do anything!" he claimed. His coat fell open, revealing the front of his shirt covered in blood.

"Well, in any case, you have some explaining to do," she told him. "Let's do that at the station."

Casey and Potts drove him, while Ellie went back to find Waters. She couldn't see him anywhere. Dana Jacobs was gone as well.

"Okay, Detective, are we done here?"

It took Ellie a moment to realize the medical examiner was talking to her. She sounded impatient too.

"Can we move the body?"

"Didn't Detective Waters say anything?"

"Not to me, no. So?"

Ellie felt uncomfortably hot, struggling to remember everything that she'd learned for the test, and in the field while observing the detectives. That had seemed so much easier in comparison.

"I guess so...Yes. Thank you."

"Ellie, do you have a moment?" Officer Atwood asked.

"We're clear," Adams told her assistant.

Understanding that she wasn't needed here any longer, Ellie stepped aside with Officer Chris Atwood. He was one of the officers who had been assigned to look for witnesses. He was also probably the only friend Waters had in the department, as they shared political views and the occasional beer.

"You found anything?"

"There was a guy, driving his truck around the park in circles," he said. "The witness was having a picnic with her family, and they saw him a few times, said it looked like he was watching someone. They gave a pretty good description of the vehicle. Might be something."

"It could be. Thanks." They were standing close to the street that led around the park. Something came to mind. "You got the approximate time? There are no cameras in the park, but there's a traffic camera over there on the street corner. Let's get that footage."

He didn't argue, but a moment later, he asked,

"So, Homicide. How did that happen?"

She and Chris had graduated from the academy the same year. Ellie knew he was rather fond of gossip. Her friend Kate had been the subject when she'd dated Derek Henderson, and there had been some talk about her and Jordan as well. Ellie thought that the best way to deal with those antics was to let it go. They'd find something new eventually.

"What do you mean? I worked. I took the test. I waited. Here I am." She made sure to keep her words light.

"That's not what everybody says, but whatever."

"What does everybody say?"

"Doesn't matter. Cliff told me I should offer you a ride. He had to go back."

"Oh, really."

"Is that a problem?"

"No, of course not. Let's go."

For someone who had been so eager to show her the ropes, he had left her on her own quickly, but Ellie wasn't going to take the bait. If that's how Waters wanted to play it, she'd play along. She'd been thrown far worse curveballs than that—and after all, she had a suspect to interview.

"I want you to get me that footage, find the guy in the truck, and then come to me ASAP," she said, taking some comfort in Atwood bristling at the command. He'd have to get used to it. Ellie wasn't going anywhere.

Chapter Two

"Come on. Here's coffee and something for you to do so you can stop stalking the sexy lady over there."

Unfortunately, Jordan didn't have as much room to argue as she would have liked, so she settled for glaring at her partner as he handed her the coffee. Ellie and Cliff Waters had left earlier. She returned soon after him, and after a quick exchange of words, they headed for the interrogation area. Ellie had always been up to the task when a lucky break presented itself, but this was her day job now. Someone should help her ease into that new routine. Jordan didn't put that much confidence in Waters, but unfortunately, the decision was Lieutenant Carroll's, not hers.

"That's my fiancée you're talking about," she said and got up, picking up her keys and coat. "I'm only here because I had to take care of some paperwork this morning."

"Yeah, right."

"So, what's the situation?"

"Possible suicide," Derek said, now serious. "Wife found husband in the garage. It looks like he hanged himself."

Jordan winced, uncomfortably aware of the chill his words sent down her spine.

"I know. We have about twenty minutes to get there, so tell me something better. I heard the word 'fiancée.' Does that mean you finally had the guts to ask her?"

"Well, technically she asked me first, but don't tell anyone. That could mess with my reputation."

"I have no doubts. That's great news though. Congratulations."

"Thanks. Yes, it is." The thought was wonderfully calming, and besides, it helped distract her from whatever challenges might come Ellie's way on her first day.

"You set a date yet?"

"Yes. May 31st."

"You'll wait a whole year?"

"No, this year."

He whistled. "Wow, you really made up your mind, didn't you? Not a lot of time to put a registry together."

"Right...at first, we thought we might do more renovations at the house, but at the time, we needed to get into it quickly when we thought Ariel was going to live with us. Now that she can't—won't—this has taken priority. It won't be big, just friends and family."

"You put your guest list together already?"

Jordan sighed. "You're right. There isn't a lot of time."

"It's your wedding," he reminded her. "You two are happy, it's all that counts. Ellie's parents are coming?"

"There's no one on Ellie's side. Parents died years ago in a car accident."

"Wow."

Jordan had nothing left to add. The past few weeks had been highly emotional, with the two of them hoping they could adopt the teenager rescued from the dismantled Prophets of Better Days cult. Then Ariel's aunt had shown up and proven to be more than capable of taking care of her niece. Jordan and

Ellie had promised to keep in touch, and they would—but for a short time, they had hoped for something different.

They would figure out the number of invitations. For now, she had to steel herself for the sight of a man who had likely taken his own life.

The house, in front of which Derek parked a few minutes later, was in an upper middle-class neighborhood, with well-kept front lawns and porches. The Kennings' was the second-to-last in a cul-de-sac, and a squad car was parked next to the gate. The coroner was on the scene as well.

Officer Libby Marshall greeted them at the door.

"You might want to talk to Mrs. Kenning first," she said. "She's in the kitchen."

The distraught woman was in her late forties. Jordan introduced Derek and herself.

"I'm so sorry for your loss," she said.

Mrs. Kenning acknowledged her words with a barely perceptible nod.

"I knew this day would come," she said. "I knew, damn it, and he wouldn't listen to me. Look at what happened."

"What do you mean?"

Jordan sat down at the table with her while Libby directed Derek to the garage.

"That's why I called the police...I mean, you have to, anyway, right? But Dan wouldn't kill himself. I know who's responsible."

Grief could certainly cloud a person's perception, but they wouldn't leave anything to chance.

"You think your husband was murdered?"

"They made him do this. The people he worked for...he had too much of a conscience for them, and once they figured that out, they wanted him gone. I warned him!" She started sobbing, and Jordan looked around, locating a box of tissues on the counter. She set it on the table in front of Mrs. Kenning.

"I understand this is a difficult time for you, but those are serious accusations. Do you have evidence that someone had a hand in—"

"That's your job, right?"

"Help me do it. Tell me what you know."

"He got this new job, about two years ago. At first, everything was great. We bought this house, we were talking about a vacation...but then, something changed. He changed. He was always working late, and when he was home, he was distracted. I thought he was having an affair. A few months ago, I confronted him, and he told me. They were forcing him to take part in illegal activities. Dan said it would be better if I didn't know too much, if the police ever questioned me. I told him to get out, that the money wasn't worth it. He said it was too late."

"Who was his employer?"

"Andrews Secure Living."

Jordan had received the occasional flyer from the firm even though the sticker on her mailbox clearly stated "no solicitation."

"We will ask some questions, I promise you."

"I hope you do. They are evil. We were married for fifteen years, detective. We finally moved into a quiet and secure neighborhood, zero crime, and...I don't know what to do now!"

"Do you have any friends or family you could stay with?" Jordan asked softly.

"This is a crime scene, right? I could stay with a friend, I suppose. I'll call her."

"You do that. We'll keep in touch," she said, laying her hand over the woman's.

"Thank you, Detective."

Jordan and Derek drove back to the station in silence. They would have to wait on test results and reports, not to mention, the autopsy, but at a first look, there was no reason to suggest foul play. Except, if Mrs. Kenning was right, someone had driven Daniel Kenning to this desperate step, placed him into a situation where he could only think of suicide as a way out. Some research was in order before they contacted his employer's local office. She also wanted to check in with Ellie quickly.

The image of Daniel Kenning haunted her, not so much the actual sight, but what it implied. Some people would never experience what it felt like to stand so close to the precipice—but at one time, a short, dark period in her life, she had. No actual plans, no actions, but the memory was enough to spook her.

❦

"Hey, Harding, wait a second."

Her hand on the door handle, Ellie turned around.

"Yes?" She hadn't mentioned her annoyance with Waters over leaving her at the scene, determined to let these first few days go by as smoothly as possible. That didn't mean she would let him walk all over her. She and Potts had arrested the suspect, twenty-seven-year-old Marco Raynor. She had faced criminals in an interrogation room before.

"I'll talk to him. Just listen."

"But—"

"You heard me."

"Fine." She was proud of herself for not snapping. They both went inside, and Waters introduced them. As much as she disagreed with him, "Detective Harding" still had a new and exciting ring to it. Ellie suppressed a smile, before she made herself focus on the situation at hand. She noticed the man in the bloody shirt was shaking. His composure clearly showed fear.

"Whose blood is that on your shirt?" Waters asked.

"Am I being charged with something? If you're not charging me, you have to let me go, right? I didn't do anything!"

"You ran from the police, after showing up in a place where a homeless woman was found with her skull caved in." Waters barely raised his voice. "I bet it's her blood, and the moment we have proof, son, we have no reason to let you go—so why don't you tell us the truth?"

"It is the truth! I didn't kill her...Lea...I found her." A tear was sneaking out of the corner of his eye.

"So you knew her. Lea. Do you have a last name?"

Waters cleared his throat. Ellie couldn't find anything wrong with her intervention, especially when Raynor said, "We didn't talk much. She was around...I saw her at the shelter a few times."

Perhaps someone from the staff would be able to provide them with a last name, so they could figure out if there was any family to notify.

"You were both homeless?" Ellie asked.

"That's obvious, isn't it?" Waters snapped. "Why don't you tell us what happened? I promise my colleague won't interrupt again."

Raynor cast an uncertain look at Ellie before he looked back at the older detective.

"It was raining pretty hard last night, so I wanted to go to the shelter. I saw Lea..." He swallowed hard. "At first, I thought she might have fallen and slipped, but I realized pretty soon that someone stabbed her. I tried to stop the bleeding, but it didn't work, and then I realized...It was already too late, anyway."

"Did anyone see you?"

"I don't think so. It was dark. Not many people were out."

"Why didn't you come to the police right away?"

14

Raynor looked at Waters as if he had said something outrageous.

"Are you kidding me? This is exactly what I was afraid of. I just came back this morning to make sure you found her, and that you're looking for the person who did this to her. Right now, you're looking at the wrong guy."

"Did you know a Willie Potter?" Ellie wasn't sure Waters would ask about the other homeless man.

There was a knock on the door, and Officer Atwood peeked inside. "Detective Harding?"

"Go," Waters said. "I'll finish up here."

She stepped outside with Chris Atwood, wondering if she'd ever get an answer to that question.

"About that guy driving around the park. A truck matching the description shows up a few times in the footage. I got a license plate, and I have a name."

"Great. Who is it?

"Bob Stanton, got arrested once for carrying without a license."

"All right, thanks. Send everything to me, please, and I'll take a look in a minute."

Before Ellie had a chance to go back inside, Waters joined them.

"He's hiding something," he said, casting a look at Raynor who, behind the two-way mirror, was fidgeting in his chair.

"I agree, but I don't think he killed her."

Waters winked at Atwood as if enjoying a shared joke.

"Listen to Harding, she has it figured out already. I can retire right now."

"I didn't mean..." Ellie felt her cheeks grow warm.

"What do you have?" Waters asked, and it took her a moment to realize he hadn't spoken to her.

"A possible witness," Atwood answered.

"Good job. Harding, what are you waiting for?"

Chapter Three

The CEO for Andrews Secure Living wasn't around, but his second-in-command reacted shocked at the news.

"Oh my God, that's terrible," he said. "I don't even know what to say. Of course we'll have to extend our condolences to Mrs. Kenning. I didn't hire him, I wasn't here yet when he started working here, so I don't know him that well. Anyway. It's a tragedy."

"You have a high turnover in the company?" Jordan asked.

He shrugged. "I don't see what that has to do with Mr. Kenning's death, but if you must know, it's no different from others. Some are temp workers—they move on. We have a dedicated regular staff, and we're committed to selling a product of the highest standard. Mr. Kenning was in sales...pretty successful, I believe. I can't even begin to imagine why he would do such a thing. Personal problems maybe?"

"Do you know if he was close with anyone in the company, someone he might have mentioned anything to?"

He shook his head in response to Derek's question. When he realized that they were waiting for more, he elaborated, "Not that I'm aware of. He attended meetings, worked long hours. There wasn't a lot of time for socializing."

So far, there wasn't much to sustain the grieving widow's theory, however, Jordan had found in her research that the company had suffered from financial problems. About two years ago, a new CEO came in, put his name in the logo, and shortly after, the company started to thrive. That, at least, was what she had been able to come up with so far.

"A while ago, the company wasn't doing well. What changed?"

"As I've told you, I wasn't here at the time, but I can tell you what happened—we updated our product line, modernized it, and we became competitive again. I'm sorry, Detective, but there's nothing shady about it."

"Oh, I didn't say that." Jordan wondered about this choice of words. "Do you know if he had been working on a big project lately, something that might have put a lot of pressure on him?"

"Detective." His tone changed. Jordan braced herself. "I'll forgive you this line of questioning because you obviously don't know much about our field. I can assure you, everyone working for Andrews Secure Living chose to be here. We don't ask anything impossible from our employees, but we demand commitment. If Mr. Kenning had problems that made him unable to fulfill his tasks, I'm sorry, but I wasn't aware of it. Anyone alleging anything else is lying. It's sad, but that's all there is."

"Very well. Thank you for your time."

Derek was about to say something when they were outside the door, but Jordan's cell phone rang, so she excused herself.

"Hello?"

"Jordan. It's so good to hear your voice. You haven't called in a while." Kathryn sounded a bit too chipper for her liking.

"I've been busy. In fact, I am at work right now. Is there anything..."

"I'd like you to come by for dinner sometime this week. And bring Ellie, too. Have you asked her yet?"

That was too much all at once, Jordan decided. The truth was she had avoided talking to her birthmother, because the subject of the marriage proposal would inevitably come up. With Kathryn, Jordan wasn't worried about her reputation. She was worried that the decision whether or not to invite her and her husband Jim might be taken right out of Jordan's hands.

"I can't talk right now," she said. "I'll let you know about dinner."

Back at the station, she went straight to the restroom and splashed some cold water on her face, frowning at her bleary reflection in the mirror.

She had no reason to feel this restless and anxious. She had done everything she could to slay her demons, and now she was going to marry Ellie, live together in the home they had chosen. Ariel was in good hands.

Jordan even managed to maintain some sort of relationship with Kathryn, keeping her at bay at the same time. Why now? She had dealt with nightmares before and understood them as a way to work through events, but there was nothing left to work through about her childhood. It was what it was, no doing better next time.

She couldn't go back and tell the child that eventually, everything would be okay—so that child kept bugging her adult self, in crystal clear nightmare images. It was exhausting and unnecessary.

"Give it a rest," she mumbled before turning away from the mirror abruptly.

Jordan wasn't entirely sure who she was talking to. She just hoped it would work.

They were standing on the porch of the one-story house where Bob Stanton, the man who had been circling the park in his vehicle, lived. His mother, Marjorie, was listed as the owner.

"Okay, Harding, you think you can handle this guy?" Waters asked.

"Sure. Not a problem." Ellie rang the doorbell, and a moment later, the man in question opened the door.

Bob Stanton was a big man sporting a buzz cut, tattoos sneaking out from underneath the sleeves of his T-shirt. Ellie wouldn't let appearances deter her. In the past few years on the job, she had met men wearing suits and a polite smile, who literally had skeletons in their closet.

"Mr. Stanton? I'm Detective Harding, this is Detective Waters. This is your vehicle?" she pointed to the truck in the driveway.

"Yes, why?" He looked her up and down.

"You were driving around Patton Lake Park yesterday? People saw you circling the park several times?"

"Is that against the law?"

"We found the body of a woman this morning. You might have seen something."

He frowned. "Like what? I see a lot of things, and I don't like them. You guys do nothing about the loitering and the beggars harassing the tourists."

"Is that why you drive by the park? Are you doing something about it?"

"Hey, lady, watch that mouth of yours." He took a step forward, irritated when Ellie wouldn't budge.

"It's Detective, and I'm not accusing you of anything." Yet, remained unspoken. "I just asked you a question."

For the first time, he looked a bit uncertain. "I'm part of a neighborhood watch, all right?"

"You carry a gun?"

"Yes, I'm a law-abiding citizen who wants to protect himself, Detective." His emphasis made the word sound like a slur. He didn't mention his record. "I have a license. You want to see it?"

"I'd like to," Ellie said in the most pleasant tone she could muster.

Bob Stanton stepped aside to let them in, and he went to a cabinet in the living room to retrieve the paperwork.

"While we're here," Waters finally spoke, "I'd like to show you some pictures, and please tell me if you noticed any of these men yesterday."

Stanton saw no reason to challenge a request made to him by a male cop. Ellie suppressed a sigh, as she was just as interested in the answer.

Looking at one picture after the other, he shook his head. "Those hobos all look the same to me. Wait—this one."

"You remember him?" Ellie asked.

"I sure do, he always begs the tourists for money. I told him several times to stay away. He was definitely there yesterday. I saw him a couple of times."

"Did you get out of the car, talk to him?"

"No, it was raining already. But I'm pretty sure that when I saw him the second time, he was carrying something heavy."

Ellie exchanged a look with her partner. One way or another, they were on to something. Bob Stanton had just identified Marco Raynor.

"I told you he was going to stay with us a little while longer," Waters told her when they were back in the car. "Everyone's telling you you're good. I'm not saying it's not true, but you can't beat experience."

"I suppose that's true."

Ellie wasn't at all convinced that Stanton was telling the truth.

Jordan had no reason to be present during the autopsy of the homeless woman found dead this morning. None that she could easily sell, anyway. She hoped that ME Melissa Adams wouldn't call her bluff, though the looks that the woman sent her way spoke volumes. Ellie had been surprised to see her here, while Waters' only reaction was a grunt. So far, so good.

Ellie seemed to be doing okay. Her own stomach was fluttering a bit at the sight of the woman's head. Aside from the two obvious injuries, a blunt object to the back of the head, and the stab wound, she appeared to have been beaten all over.

"I looked at the file of the man who died last month, Willie Potter. He had some older bruises too," Ellie said.

"Not that again." Waters groaned. "ME already ruled out a homicide. Guy was malnourished and hypothermic when he died. End of story."

Ellie straightened her shoulders and took a closer look at the body on the table. She was a bit pale, Jordan noticed, but holding up nicely.

Jordan barely suppressed a proud smile.

"Detective Carpenter, don't you have someplace to be? I won't be getting to your guy until tomorrow, I'm afraid."

Ellie cast her a quick smile to let her know she'd seen through her as well.

Jordan shrugged.

"Fine. I'll see you later, then."

When she went back to her desk, she found Derek sitting at his, amused.

"Someone called your bluff?"

"What? I went to ask Melissa when we can expect her report."

"And you had to do that in person. Liar. I take it Ellie didn't faint during the first autopsy she witnessed?"

"No, of course not. Would you leave it be?"

"All right." Derek pushed his chair back. "I think we should talk to the CEO as well. He and his former business partner were accused of embezzling big sums of money, but the charges fell apart all of a sudden. He went on to head Andrews Secure Living. Get this, the partner killed himself."

"Whoa. This company has some seriously bad mojo. Why didn't number two tell us about it?"

"More like bad *guys*, and that's the million-dollar question. CEO isn't back until the day after tomorrow. By then, we should have all the results."

"Yeah." She stared at her own screen with a sigh. "I wish we had something solid to tell the wife."

"We might get there soon. Doesn't look as cut and dried as it did a few hours ago."

Jordan wasn't sure if the truth was going to set this man's widow free, but they were going to find it, in any case—if not today.

Tomorrow night, they were going to see Ariel. Maybe by tomorrow, she'd also have figured out what to tell Kathryn, about dinner and the wedding day.

⁂

Raynor had been assigned a public defender who advised him not to talk to the police anymore, and that seemed to be the end of it as far as Waters was concerned. Ellie thought she had to share her theories at least.

"Let it go," he advised. "That other case is not related. Maria and I worked on it. We closed it. As for Mr. Neighborhood

Watch, he has no reason to lie to us. He knows we'll take a closer look because of his record."

Ellie nodded, though she wasn't convinced. Bob Stanton didn't appear worried about being questioned by the police at all, in fact, he'd acted rather cocky.

After Waters had left, she sat at her desk and wrote down some notes. *Ask Raynor about Willie Potter.* She had convinced reluctant witnesses before. She also wanted to talk to some employees at the park tourist office, to get a feel for who had the bigger secrets, Stanton or Raynor. If she was lucky, she could get all of this done before Waters found out. If it didn't lead to anything, he never had to.

In the parking lot, she met Detective Rogers from Missing Persons. He waved to her, then locked his car again and came over.

"Congratulations on your promotion." After a small pause, he asked, "Have you heard from McCarthy?"

Kate McCarthy, one of Ellie's closest friends, had decided to leave the force after working with Rogers on a particularly grueling case.

"Yes. She's doing fine now." Ellie wasn't sure how much Rogers really knew, about Kate losing her fiancé, then dating Derek Henderson and breaking up with him. She had put lots of determination into finding a missing woman who had turned up dead.

"When is she coming back?"

Kate had left town abruptly to live and work with her grandparents. When Ellie had last seen her, she had implied that she might come back sometime soon, but not to the job.

"I'm not sure, but I don't think she wants to be a cop anymore."

"I don't blame her." He sighed. "It's a shame, though. She was good. Sometimes, things don't work out. Thanks for letting me know. Have a good night."

"You too. Bye."

Ellie sat in her car for a moment, telling herself she had nothing to feel guilty about.

She and Kate had made different choices. That was all.

Still, it felt good to arrive at the familiar table at the *Night Shift* and be greeted with cheers.

Jordan had endured some good-natured ribbing for sneaking into the autopsy. She pulled Ellie close for a kiss before they sat in the booth.

"You made it. Congratulations."

"Thank you. I couldn't have done it without you."

Ellie wasn't sure why that produced some laughter from the group of her friends. "Come on, I'm serious. All of you. I'm paying for this round, too, how about that?"

"Careful, baby," Jordan said. "We just bought a house, and we have to invite all of these people to our wedding."

Apparently, there were some of them who hadn't heard the news yet.

It occurred to Ellie that this was where she'd always wanted to be, professionally and personally. The moment was here. If it seemed a little too good to be true, she didn't care. She had paid her dues, they both had.

Time to be happy.

Chapter Four

"M*om, I'm hungry."*

The woman sitting at the picnic table, holding on to a bottle, didn't seem to care much. It was unclear whether she was even listening.

"Mom..."

"Go over to Christine's and ask her."

"I don't have time. I have to go to school."

"Then make yourself something, for God's sake! You're old enough!"

Jordan sat up in bed, wiping a hand across her face, glad that she hadn't woken Ellie. Gradually, she let reality comfort her. This was her life. Nothing to worry about, least of all those little snippets her subconscious conjured up these days, slivers of a time long gone.

They were distracting and frustrating, at best. Why now? She had done all she could, opened the door to Kathryn so they could both be adults and live in the present. Maybe dinner wasn't a good idea. Maybe she had made a mistake thinking she and Kathryn could ever have something real, and untainted.

"Are you okay?" Ellie asked softly.

Jordan lay back down and let herself be embraced. "I didn't want to wake you," she mumbled.

"Can't sleep?"

"It's no big deal," Jordan said, not wanting anything to overshadow this important day for Ellie. "Kathryn wants us to come by for dinner."

"Of course I'll come with you. There's strength in numbers."

Jordan couldn't help but laugh. "That's not it. She knows about the wedding, or at least suspects. I'm not sure I want her there."

Ellie was silent for a moment, but Jordan could easily read her mind. She would have given anything if her parents could be present. That was different though. Ellie's memories of her family weren't fraught with neglect.

"What would you need to feel better about it?"

"Tricky. I would need her to have been a different person back then."

"You're worried about what Jack and Pauline might think? I'm sure they wouldn't mind. I wouldn't mind either."

"So it's decided then." She hadn't meant for her words to sound so harsh.

"No," Ellie said calmly. "You decide. I promise you, whatever it is, I will support you."

"Thank you. I'm sorry. This was a big day for you."

"Yes, and it's only the beginning. Like the wedding. Remember that the guests will only be there for a day, but you're stuck with me forever."

Jordan turned to her. "That sounds wonderful."

"Yeah?" Ellie's smile was all promise. "Try to relax a bit. I can help you with that."

It was an offer Jordan didn't want to refuse, even though they both had an early morning coming up.

Ellie had left the house while Jordan was still in the shower, but she'd brewed a fresh pot of coffee first.

Raynor was first on her list—the park's tourist service wasn't open yet. On her way, she pondered the progress they'd made on the case so far.

Ellie had made it through the autopsy with her dignity intact, horrified by the implications of the injuries rather than the sight of them.

They still didn't have more than the first name, Lea. The woman's body was bruised all over. The rain had washed away most of the evidence, but a pattern of broken branches seemed to point to Ellie's theory. They had toyed with her. Perhaps she'd been able to run, and they came after her, finishing with hitting her in the head, with a rock, likely. Not that they had found said object, or the knife.

She hoped Raynor, who was still waiting for his arraignment, would be able to help fill in some of the blanks. He seemed surprised to see her.

"Why do you want to talk to me?" he asked, his resignation obvious. "You made up your mind, didn't you?"

"I have a few more questions, if you don't mind."

"Does it matter?"

"Do you know someone named Willie Potter?"

Ellie could tell that she was on to something before he answered. His eyes widened, and he avoided his gaze.

"Marco, I'm not out to get you. Two people died within a few weeks, and I'm trying to find out who's responsible."

"Willie died of exposure. I heard talk about it at the shelter," he clarified. "I'm not surprised the police wasn't looking too hard."

"What do you mean?"

"Just another bum off the streets, right?"

Ellie straightened in her chair. "You also seem to assume that everyone's the same. I'm here now. I'm listening to you."

"Yeah, not like that's going to help me. Either I go to jail, or they get to me too."

"Who?"

"I don't know!" He raked a hand through his hair. "Some guys, looking for trouble. Willie told me they started beating him up without reason, just like that."

"Did he tell you what they looked like? Anything that would help us to identify them?"

Raynor shook his head. "You might care, but it's not enough. Some higher up will assign you to a more important case, and others will get killed."

"That's not going to happen, I swear."

"It was dark. He said they were all wearing dark sweaters, one of them had some lettering on it."

"What kind? Like from a company?"

"He didn't know. Willie couldn't read."

Ellie suppressed a curse. The picture unfolding got worse by the minute, and Waters thought the case was closed. "Look, if you want me to help you, you need to help me. A witness saw you that night, around the time of the murder, carrying something heavy."

"Like what? That isn't true. I told you already I found Lea, but I couldn't save her. I knew this was gonna happen!"

"There's not going to be another murder. We do care, and we will find out who killed Lea, and, possibly Willie, okay?"

"Why do you care?" he muttered, though she had seen the hope flicker in his eyes.

"I'm not the only one. It's our job to keep all people in the city safe."

I'm not the exception, she thought. Cliff Waters is.

It was too late to drive by the park's office, so Ellie decided to meet with her partner and discuss the next steps based on what she'd found. She saw Jordan and Derek exiting the lieutenant's office. Detective Waters was at his desk, getting to his feet when she came in.

"Harding, let's go. The A.D.A. is here."

"Already? We weren't..." She broke off her sentence when Waters knocked on Lieutenant Carroll's door, and they both walked in.

"Morning, sir," he greeted their supervisor, addressing A.D .A. Esposito with a nod.

"Good morning," she said curtly. "On your suspect..."

"He hasn't confessed, but we have a witness that places him at the scene. He doesn't even deny he was there, gave us some story why her blood was all over him, claims he wanted to help her. He's hiding something."

"Well, yeah, that's circumstantial at best," Esposito said doubtfully. "What about your witness?"

"If I may..." Ellie ventured. "Yes, he was hiding something, but he talked to me this morning. He's scared. It's possible that Willie Potter was murdered as well, and Marco Raynor is afraid he could be next."

She wasn't surprised by Waters' audible groan. "What part of 'let it go' didn't you understand? That case is closed. If Raynor had any suspicions, why didn't he come forward?"

"Detective Harding?" the lieutenant prompted.

Ellie had to admit she was still a bit startled when addressed like this. After all, it was only the second day.

"Yes. I thought it was important to ask him about the other victim, since it happened in the same area, and we didn't have the time yesterday. I think he's truly scared. As for why he didn't come forward, they didn't exactly check in with each other. Raynor learned about Potter's death at the shelter. He says that Potter told him about a group of men that had beaten him. They were wearing sweatshirts with lettering—he couldn't describe any of the men though."

"Convenient," Waters muttered.

"He said he wasn't carrying anything heavy."

"About the witness." Ellie turned to A.D.A. Esposito. "I ran a check on him. His ex-wife filed charges last year after a domestic dispute. The charges were dropped, because she never appeared in court...but I imagine that kind of thing would come up."

"I'd certainly make sure we know about it before we put him on the stand," Valerie Esposito agreed. "Congratulations on the new job, by the way."

"Oh...thanks."

"Yeah, well, part of a new job is to listen to people who've been doing this for a while."

Valerie smiled. "True, Cliff, but a pair of fresh eyes is always helpful. I'd hesitate to rely on a likely domestic abuser to testify in a case where a woman was violently murdered."

"Alleged domestic abuser."

"You're right," Lieutenant Carroll agreed, "but it still doesn't look good. If you're sure Raynor is our man, find a better witness, or evidence to support your theory. If not, well, then find me the real killer. We don't want people to think we're treating one murder case differently from another."

"Thank you, sir," Ellie said. "I also meant to talk to the park employees once more—maybe they remember something, either about the witness or Raynor."

"You do that."

"We're done here?" Esposito asked. "That's not a whole lot you people give me to work with."

"What do you want? He probably threw the rock and the knife into the lake."

"Come back when you have proof."

Ellie hadn't expected Waters to be happy with the actions she had taken, but she hoped now that it moved them forward slightly, he might be more forgiving.

She'd been wrong.

"We need to talk," he said once they had exited the lieutenant's office.

"Okay. Sure."

Ellie followed him to the break room. He waited until she was inside, and then slammed the door shut hard enough to make her flinch.

"What the hell were you thinking?"

"I'm sorry, but there was no time to tell you. I didn't want to rush anything, and I thought Raynor could tell us something about Willie Potter. It turned out he could. I'm thinking we also could ask around in shelters, see if they heard about someone being threatened..."

"We will do all of these things. I know you'll do whatever you can to get ahead, but you have to understand something. You're not the first person to do the job. You think you know everything, but being that cocky could get somebody killed someday."

Ellie kept her head up thinking that rushing ahead to declare someone guilty wasn't any less cocky. She kept that thought to herself.

"You show me up again like that, and you'll be in trouble."

"I understand," she said calmly.

"Do you?"

The door opened, and Derek Henderson walked inside.

"Everything all right in here?" he asked.

"We're fine," Ellie hurried to say.

"Okay." In the resulting uncomfortable silence, he got himself a coffee and left.

"Come on, let's go. We'll have a couple of uniforms go to the shelters, and let's see what the park employees have to say."

Perhaps she was a bit spooked, but to Ellie, it sounded like he wanted to make it look like he had just come up with these ideas. Working with this man was without a doubt a challenge. She was up to it.

***

"Thank you," Jordan said when Derek returned from the impromptu assignment she had given him. They were going to meet with the CEO of Andrews Secure Living next. The autopsy results weren't in yet. Mrs. Kenning had called and asked to be updated.

"You know you can't be around all the time," Derek said when they were in the car. "If you keep sending me instead of doing the hovering yourself, she'll figure that out too. She's a detective, you know."

"Come on, stop it. It was just one time. Waters has been such a jerk to Doss, and you know it. I want to know if he's doing the same thing to Ellie."

"And you're going to do what? He has his moments, no doubt, but he's not stupid. He's not going to do anything to endanger his retirement." Derek shrugged. "Though I doubt he'll be happier, but that's none of my business or yours. How are the wedding plans coming along?"

"They're coming along."

"That's all?"

"Speaking of which, have you talked to Kate? Could we seat you two together, or is that not a good idea?"

"Okay, you got me there. Same table is fine. We're adults."

"Maria too?"

"Stop it now. I get it, no more talk about personal lives. Let's see what Mr. Andrews has to say."

Jordan was fine with that. Last night's talk with Ellie had been helpful, but she still didn't know what to do about Kathryn. The distraction was most welcome.

The CEO of Andrews Secure Living was a busy man according to his secretary. Earlier on the phone, he had promised he'd be available, but now, the woman with the perfectly manicured nails claimed she couldn't reach him anywhere.

"You could come back later," she suggested.

"That's fine, thank you. We'll wait."

This was nothing but a silly power play, Jordan assumed, trying to tell them that his time was more valuable than anyone else's.

After about twenty minutes, the CEO arrived and asked them into his office.

"My apologies I'm late, but I'm afraid I have to cut our meeting short as well."

Jordan cast a quick look at Derek. *Told you so.*

"This won't take long," she said.

"It's about Kenning, right? Such a sad story. I can't help feeling bad. I wonder if we're partly responsible."

"Why would that be?" Derek asked.

"I assume you know we had to fire him. His work performance had been sub par for a while now, and as much as we sympathized, I had to act in the best interest of the company."

"How did he handle it when you told him?"

"He seemed...fine. Of course, the problems at home didn't go away, and I imagine that's the main reason he did it."

"What kind of problems are you talking about?"

"His wife? She had mental problems. Paranoia. He had to take days off to take care of her. I suppose it all got too much for him. Such a shame."

"How do you know all this?" After meeting Mrs. Kenning, Jordan wasn't yet ready to believe in this completely different version of the story, especially given Andrews' history with his partner.

"When I realized his work was suffering, I had to ask him, but I promised him not to tell anyone. Obviously, these are different circumstances. The poor woman. I hope she has family to take care of her."

"Before you started Andrews Secure Living, you worked with a partner named...Larry Ferguson?"

"Yes, why? That has nothing to do with poor Mr. Kenning."

"Can you tell us about the circumstances of Mr. Ferguson's death?"

"He killed himself. Come on, Detectives, I can't believe what you're insinuating here. It's an unfortunate coincidence."

"We're not insinuating anything," Derek assured him. "This must be a difficult time for you."

"It certainly is, but there was no relation between the two. Larry was single, and he seemed happy. No one ever knew why he did it. Mr. Kenning, now, that's another story. Why are you even here? You don't think someone staged his suicide?"

"We are trying to understand what happened."

"Yeah, well, let me know if you find out. I need to go. Is that all?"

"Yes, thank you. We'll be in touch."

Back in the car, Jordan saw she had a text from Dr. Adams. *I'm working on my report right now,* it said, *but don't expect too much. No proof of outside influence.*

"Does that make you feel better or worse?" Derek asked when she told him.

"I'm not sure. I need coffee. I can't think."

"Stayed up past your bedtime last night?"

"None of your business. Over there," she pointed at the coffee shop sign. "We can brainstorm meanwhile."

"Looks like it's over. What's to talk about?"

Jordan wasn't sure. Something still didn't sit right with her. At the same time, she was afraid the CEO might have told the truth about Mrs. Kenning.

"That's why they call it brainstorming. If there's something to find, we'll find it."

By the time she watched Ellie getting ready for the evening at the Cranes', Ariel's aunt and uncle that had taken her in, Jordan still wasn't sure what to think of the case. It stayed at the back of her mind. She found it hard to switch to off-time...though Ellie sitting in front of the mirror, putting on make-up with a sure hand, helped.

"We're not late, are we?" she asked, aware of Jordan's scrutiny.

"No. I just like watching you."

In the mirror, Ellie gave her a smile. "You want me to do you?"

Jordan coughed, even as Ellie held up the small tube of mascara.

"Oh. Okay. I was talking about this. I don't think we'd have the time for what you're implying."

"Yeah...That's okay. I'll wait for you downstairs," Jordan said, quickly making her retreat. Ellie was still laughing.

Chapter Five

S eeing Ariel always came with many mixed emotions. Most importantly, Ellie was grateful that the girl had found a family that gave her a safe place to thrive. For a brief moment, she and Jordan had thought they could offer her that space. Then along came Becca Crane, a surgeon who had been out of the country to help in poorer places in the world. She had a husband, and a daughter who was a couple of years younger than Ariel, all of them excited about the new addition to the family. A perfect happy ending.

Sitting at the table with the Crane family was still a tad awkward, but of course it was up to the adults to keep the big picture in mind, to give some peace to a girl who had grown up in a highly abusive environment and was still grieving her mother. At the same time, the Cranes had to give their younger daughter the context she needed, in a way that was appropriate for her age.

"So, how's school?" Jordan asked. It was a fairly safe question—they knew from Rebecca Crane that Ariel was doing well. Studying seemed to be a welcome distraction, and while girls' education hadn't been a priority for the cult, her mother Deborah had made sure she was up to date for her grade level.

Ariel shrugged. "It's okay. I wish people would stop asking me what it was like. They think it's like some movie." She straightened. "It's all right though. Confusing. We didn't have a lot of music and stuff...back then."

She was wearing jeans and a T-shirt now, her hair in a ponytail. When they'd found her, she'd been wearing the same shapeless dress and the braided hairstyle that was customary for women living with the Prophets of Better Days.

"Mariah is helping me catch up," she added, making the younger girl blush. "I've seen some of my siblings—my other siblings—as well, and Dad's other wives. Many of them are doing better now."

"I'm glad. I'm sure it was good to talk to them."

"Oh yes. I want to write a book, to warn others. Rebecca promised to help me."

"That's great," Jordan said, but Ellie had caught the hint of alarm in her voice. There was something she needed to clear up.

Ariel bonding with her new family was a good thing. A book, much like the one that had prompted the cult founder to order Jennifer Beaumont killed, wasn't, in Jordan's opinion. Not that the Prophets of Better Days had much reach these days, but she didn't think Ariel was ready to tackle such a project. She finally had the time and space to be a teenager, free of the worry that she would have to become a wife any day.

"I know what you want to say," Becca Crane said when they were standing in the kitchen, waiting for the coffee to brew. "I was worried too, but we talked with the therapist, and she said it might actually help her. We'll take it slow, nothing that will interfere with her homework or Mariah's pop culture lessons, I promise."

"Ariel was and is in a unique position, because her mother helped her see through the lies and smokescreens. She feels responsible, but someone has to show her that there are boundaries. She is not an adult. She's not the one who has to fix what the adults in her life messed up—and with her testimony, she already went above and beyond."

"I completely agree, Jordan," Becca said patiently, and it occurred to Jordan that she might have crossed a line.

"I'm sorry."

"I am not. I'm happy that you feel protective of her, and that we can talk about these things. We want the same thing."

"Yes, we do. And contrary to what it might look like, I didn't come here to question your choices. In fact, Ellie and I are going to get married next month, and we'd like you to come."

Up until a few weeks ago, they had been strangers. Why was this so easy, and so much more complicated when it came to her own birthparents?

"That's great, congratulations. We'd love to, and I'm sure Ariel will be excited."

At first, they had thought getting married would be helpful when trying to adopt Ariel, but now that it wasn't going to happen, they had realized that this was what they wanted, still.

"Good. You'll keep us up to date on how it's going with the book? There might be some legal ramifications as well."

"Yes, of course. We'll make sure everything is taken care of. Ariel is safe with us."

"Thank you."

⁂

The next morning, Jordan didn't have any more time to hover, as she sat across from Mrs. Kenning in her living room, telling her that she could claim her husband's body now that the autopsy was done.

"I am so sorry," she said. "There was nothing to suggest any outside influence."

"No!" There were tears in her eyes, but she wiped her face angrily. "You weren't listening to me. Those people had a hand in it."

Paranoia?

"I know it's a lot to deal with."

"First of all, you need to deal with the people who got him killed!"

"I spoke to his employer. They said his work performance had suffered lately, and that there were other things on his mind."

She laughed bitterly, shaking her head. "You don't have to be so polite about it. Andrews wants to blame the crazy wife? I figured. I'll tell you the truth. I had some problems, years ago, and it was hard on our marriage. I found a therapist, got the right medication, and I've been doing much better since. It's bullshit. None of this ever influenced his work performance."

"I can have my colleagues in another division look into the firm, but I'm really sorry. I agree that it's wrong for them to talk about you and your husband like that, but unfortunately, there's nothing I can do about it. You could probably sue for libel."

"What if I show you evidence?"

"Can you?"

"No," she said as the tears started falling faster. "Please. He was a good man. Don't give up yet."

"If you can think of anything, call me," Jordan said, wondering if she might regret that promise.

"You have to admit it's a strange coincidence," Derek said when they were sitting in the break room over a coffee, musing about the ending of the case.

"I talked to the ME in Benton County about the Ferguson case. No evidence of foul play either. Sometimes, people want to end it."

"That some fatalistic talk for a woman about to get married."

"Yeah, well, I'm in a good place now. I wasn't always, and I remember what it was like to have no hope..." Jordan held up a hand when she saw the alarm on her partner's face. "That was a long time ago. All I'm saying is people don't always see it, not even the ones close to you. The world closes in on you."

"Wow. I don't know what to say."

"You don't have to say anything...but you might want to go a little easier on Bethany the next time you see her." This wasn't the time and place. Jordan wasn't sure there would ever be a time and place to bring up this subject with him, but she'd known the moment would come when they first caught the Kenning case. "Like I said, it was a long time ago. I'm getting married. Life is pretty amazing."

"Yeah. And you don't have to invite anyone you don't want there." Derek had caught on quickly.

"Fortunately. I guess I'll go finish my report now. That poor woman will be left with many questions—and I don't think she has the means or the energy to sue Andrews for libel."

"It's sad, but there's nothing else we can do for her," Derek reminded her.

"That's what I told her, and it felt pretty crappy. All right. Let's get to work."

Even though Waters had agreed they should interview the park employees, Ellie couldn't help thinking he wasn't going to change his mind about Raynor. On the bright side, his barely concealed disinterest allowed her to take the lead.

"Yeah, I've seen him before," the young park employee said when Ellie showed her Marco Raynor's picture. "He's been around…A couple of times, I had to ask him to leave, but he was always nice about it. Not that it helped much. I didn't know the woman who died."

"Willie Potter? Does that name ring a bell?"

She shook her head when Ellie swiped to another photo on her cell. "No, I don't think I've seen him before. The older ones usually stay under the radar, don't get into fights like Mr. Raynor."

"He was picking fights?"

Ellie could have sworn there was a smug tone to Waters' voice. He overestimated how much she wanted to be right. She wanted to find Lea's killer, and make sure they hadn't made a mistake with Potter.

"Not with me," the woman said. "As I said, he was always polite to us, but he got into it with this dude a couple of times. Big guy, always going on about how the police don't do enough to protect the neighborhood from crime—sorry."

"That's all right. Go on."

"Anyway, he was carrying, and I was afraid the situation might escalate, but when I asked them both to leave, they did."

"You said it happened a couple of times? Was it that man?"

"Oh yes, definitely. He wasn't happy, called me a few names too."

"So, it was him who started the fight?"

The woman looked uncomfortable.

"Look, I can't be everywhere at every moment. I know this guy here came by every once in a while. He told Raynor to get a job. I mean...it doesn't look good when they beg the tourists, but on the other hand, it's not that easy."

"Did you ever hear Mr. Raynor threaten the other man?" Waters asked.

"Not directly, but it got pretty heated between them."

"Okay. Thank you for your time," he said and turned to leave the office. Ellie didn't have much of a choice other than to follow him.

"Stanton didn't tell us the whole truth," she said when they walked back to the car.

"Neither did Raynor."

"Yes, but...Raynor had no reason to kill Lea. Or Potter. He's clearly afraid. Stanton on the other hand...He has a history of violence, and he's carrying."

"The woman wasn't shot. Someone stabbed her and bashed her skull in."

Ellie winced at the graphic imagery. "Stanton does seem to have a problem with the homeless people in the park."

"To which he has a right. Harding, you're prejudiced about this guy."

"Maybe you're right," Ellie said instead of what was really on her mind—that a rap sheet was hardly a preconceived notion. She couldn't ignore the fact that Lea had been stabbed, though, and in Potter's case, they didn't even have proof that he'd been murdered.

She wondered if Waters would be livid if she saw Stanton one more time. It was probably fair to give him a heads-up first.

"I'd like to confirm with Stanton what the employee said."

To her surprise, he simply shrugged. "Let's see if we can cross that off the list right now."

They found Stanton taking a cigarette break outside the hardware store where he worked.

"You bring good news, I assume," he said, tossing the cigarette to the ground and putting it out with his shoe. "I hear that bum got arrested...Finally someone's doing their job."

"About that...We hoped you could help us with something. The park employee said you and Mr. Raynor got into a fight more than once. Could you tell us what they were about?"

He frowned at her, anger simmering so close to the surface she almost took a step backwards.

"I'll tell you what it was about all right!" He was in her personal space.

"Easy, buddy," Waters said in a warning tone. "You heard her. Just a few follow-up questions."

"You got your killer. What do you want from me?"

"Some employees of the park office were concerned about those altercations," Ellie said. "Did Mr. Raynor threaten you or anyone else?"

"Their presence is threatening to families and tourists, and you're just sitting on your asses."

"Hey. That's enough!"

Stanton wasn't happy with Waters' assessment, but he backed down.

"I'm trying to protect our neighborhood, that's all. Who knows, at some point they might not stop at killing one another. In any case, I'm glad you got him. That's all I have to say."

"Thanks for helping us out here. Detective Harding?"

Ellie followed Waters back to the car. Something was unfinished here, but she understood she had no more talking room.

Earlier that day, she had asked Casey and Potts to look at shelters closest to the park and see if any threats had been made, but there was no news from them yet.

"What do we do now?" she asked.

"Have lunch. Come on. They will get back to us as soon as they have something."

"Yeah." Ellie sighed.

"Remember, just because someone looks good as a subject, doesn't mean he did it. Stanton had an alibi."

She was disconcerted for other reasons. Stanton might not be their guy, but there was no doubt he had threatened people in the past, including his ex-wife. He exuded an air of self-right-eousness, mostly towards women. That, plus the fact that he was carrying a gun, worried her.

What was even worse, if Stanton wasn't the killer, and Raynor wasn't either, they had to start over.

Ellie's mood improved when they entered the diner across from the station to find Jordan and Derek had chosen it for their break as well. They were sitting at a table with Maria Doss. Derek waved them over, and Ellie pulled herself a chair, leaving the remaining seat in the booth to Waters.

"Hey. You're lucky, we just learned they changed the cook. The burgers are pretty good now."

"I'm not sure if I can get her to sit down for five minutes, but it's worth a try," Waters joked.

For the time being, Ellie enjoyed being a part of this exclusive group, marveling at how much had changed in her life, and how quickly. This was where she'd wanted to be. She had earned her place at the table—and she'd make sure she'd keep her promise to Marco Raynor.

Ellie wasn't surprised when she returned from the bathroom to find Jordan standing outside the door.

"Hey. I know what you're going to ask, but I'm fine. I'm sure it would be nicer to work with either of you, but it's not so bad. You don't have to worry."

"Actually, I wanted to ask you if you haven't changed your mind about dinner at Kathryn's."

"No, why would I? Why don't we see how the evening goes, and decide about inviting her later? Jordan?"

"Okay." She looked apologetic. "I admit it's not all about Kathryn. I saw Valerie earlier. She was quite frank about Waters' antics."

"Yeah, small world, but I told you the truth. I'll be fine. Lieutenant Carroll even agreed with me." Ellie decided it was not necessary to share the content of her conversation with Waters that had followed. "I'm not a fan either, but Waters has closed a lot of cases. I respect that."

"All right. Thanks for putting up with me."

"It's not that hard," Ellie said and leaned forward to kiss her. "I have to go back to work now."

"Yeah, me too. I'll see you later."

Jordan read over her report once more. It contained all the pieces. Nothing more to add. If she was still feeling restless, it didn't have anything to do with this case, did it? Ellie was holding her own. Mrs. Kenning would work through her grief with the support of her family and friends, and...the nightmares would stop. They had before. This was the part of her subconscious having trouble believing that good times could last, and eventually, it would shut up and let her be. After she'd made a decision.

For a moment, she let herself imagine what could happen if she invited Kathryn, maybe Jim. Jack and Pauline had no reason to doubt their place in Jordan's life, and they wouldn't, should she decide to have her birthmother and her husband at the wedding.

Jim, however, had been a rare presence in her childhood. Kathryn had been around more often, but it was hard to remember times when she wasn't drunk or stoned. Apart from that one slap she remembered, they hadn't been physically abusive, just...not available. They should understand that this day of all days was reserved for the people who had shown up for Jordan, and Ellie.

She could anticipate Kathryn's talking points, about leaving the past behind, and focusing on their relationship in the present, or maybe she was mixing up all the good advice she'd gotten from people in the past few months. She and Kathryn had been almost okay. They were communicating like adults. Conversations were less of a minefield. It was ironic that something that would be the most adult and mature decision in her life brought out a disappointed, hurt child.

"How about a drink when we're done here?" Derek asked.

Even though she was looking at the dinner with some apprehension, Jordan was equally relieved to have an excuse. Give it a few days, after all the heavy subjects that had come up today.

"Another time. Ellie and I are having dinner with Kathryn tonight."

"I see. Good luck."

"Yeah. I can use it."

Jordan found herself oddly excited when she drove home after her shift that night. Of course, that had less to do with the upcoming dinner, and everything with the fact that Ellie was waiting for her.

She had shared an apartment with Bethany for many years, and from there all but fled to a house that was too far away from work, and much too related to the worst case of her career to become a permanent home.

Permanent. This was it now, and Jordan didn't feel the slightest bit apprehensive about it. That was a big change. Only one of more to come—no reason to wait for the other shoe to drop.

Chapter Six

There was no doubt that the process of becoming reacquainted with her birthmother had been trying for Jordan. There were reasons for that, and because of those reasons, Ellie was wary of giving the woman too much leeway. At the same time, she tried to keep a bigger picture in mind. If there was any way for Jordan to benefit from the contact in the present, it was a good thing in Ellie's book, and she'd do whatever she could to support her.

Maybe she wasn't completely unselfish, wishing she could still talk to her own parents, but she thought she was mostly aware of her motives.

Kathryn was making an effort, she couldn't deny that. After stepping into the modest home, she gave the two of them space for an awkward hug that pained her to watch, initiated by Kathryn, who next shook her hand.

"Ellie. It's so nice you could come. Jim won't be here tonight, so it's a girl's night."

"I look forward to it," Ellie said, which wasn't entirely a lie. "How have you been?"

It was a valid question, given that the last time they'd met Kathryn had been in the hospital.

"I'm good. Come on in, sit. I don't drink anymore, but I thought you might like a glass of wine. Red or white? I didn't know which you prefer, so I bought both. I think the red goes better with the meal, but if you prefer—"

"Red is fine," Jordan said quickly. Ellie acknowledged that she probably didn't care if it went with the meal—whatever was nearest, would do.

"You think so too, Ellie? You can have a glass of white."

"No, thanks. I'm good with red."

It was a bit dark inside, but the table was quite cozy, with a vase of flowers at the center, and candles. She wondered what was on Jordan's mind at this moment...so many conversations they still needed to have. All of a sudden, the wedding date seemed soon. Not that Ellie had any doubt in her mind that she wanted to spend the rest of her life with Jordan. However, there was a lot she could only guess up to this point, and that information was relevant as to who should have access to this special day. She followed Kathryn into the small kitchen that could have used an update a long time ago. Then again, Kathryn and Jim didn't have the means that she and Jordan had.

"Can I help you with anything?"

"If you could take these?" Kathryn handed her the two glasses of wine she'd just poured. "I'll be with you in a minute."

Ellie went back to join Jordan who had an absentminded look on her face.

"Here. Are you okay?" she asked, dropping her voice to a whisper.

Jordan laughed self-consciously. "I guess so. This...It's surreal."

"So far so good, right?"

"I guess."

Kathryn brought bowls of salad, and while they ate, she asked, "So you're all moved in at the new house yet?"

"It's been a few weeks." Jordan's answer wasn't admonishing, just matter of fact. Ellie wasn't sure she'd ever told Kathryn that they had talked about adopting Ariel before Rebecca Crane returned from her mission.

"How are the wedding plans coming along? Did you set a date?"

"Yes, we did," Jordan said, and for a few seconds, an awkward silence ensued.

"Look, I know you probably don't want to see me there," Kathryn spoke eventually. "I wish things were different, but I understand. It's not my place to ask this of you, but you should know I'm happy for you."

"Thank you."

Ellie figured that this might be the best-case scenario. She knew Jordan had been losing sleep over this question. The only person, who could and should make this easier on her, was Kathryn.

"But I've thought about it, and...why not?" Jordan continued. "I know you're making an effort, and I'm not completely blind to that. If Ellie's all right with you coming, I am too."

There was another meaningful pause until Ellie realized she was up. "Of course."

Kathryn seemed to be taken aback by the offer. Her eyes were welling up when she said, "You can't imagine what this means to me. I...I know we can't change the past, but maybe I can be here for you right now. I have to leave you for a moment, because there's still food in the oven, and I'm afraid it's going to burn."

When she was out of earshot, Ellie turned to Jordan. She didn't need to say a word—her surprise at the turn of events was likely showing.

Jordan shrugged. "I want an end to all of this. I know she's not evil, but she's also not in a position to ask anything of me—so I had to say it."

"You're amazing. I love you," Ellie whispered before Kathryn returned with more plates.

More wine, too. Neither Ellie nor Jordan had said no to a refill, both of them overly aware of the tension that had been in the room from the moment they'd come in. It was dissipating slowly. If only she could come up with a solution for her case as well.

"This is delicious, by the way," she said. "Thank you for having us."

"I'm happy to. I've been volunteering at a non-profit restaurant for some time now—you might have heard about it. They teach you how to cook healthy as well."

"That's good. I'm glad for you." Jordan's wistful tone, given the shared past of these two women, was heartbreaking. At the same time, Ellie couldn't help feeling hopeful about the future. They were both coming to terms with the events that had shaped them.

"If you'll excuse me for a moment..."

She got up after Kathryn pointed her in the direction of the bathroom. It was a small space, but like the rest of the home, clean and well-kept, though undeniably dated.

Turning around, she accidentally knocked over the box that held the replacement toilet paper.

"Clumsy," she chided herself, as she picked up box, lid, the toilet paper roll and...something else. "Oh no." If this felt like a gut punch to her, how would Jordan react? As the seconds ticked by, Ellie entertained the thought of not telling her. The evening had gone surprisingly well so far, and she didn't want to spoil it. Then again, Jordan had a right to know. Keeping secrets, even with the best of intentions, had never served them. Right here and now was not the moment, though. Ellie put everything back where she'd found it and returned to the table.

Jordan and Kathryn were laughing about something, a joke that she'd missed. Ellie wanted to cry.

She felt worse by the minute. Jordan was unusually chatty on the drive home.

"Thank you for pushing me a little," she said. "I think this was important. The job doesn't always make it easy to believe that people can change. Has she? I don't know, but in any case, with all her misgivings, she's not evil." It was the second time that night Jordan used the term evil, Ellie noted.

"No, she's not. That doesn't mean your side of the story changes."

"No, it doesn't," Jordan agreed. "But it's this woman you saw tonight that's coming to the wedding...not a drugged out irresponsible parent. I think I can handle this, and it's mostly because of you. God, I love you so much."

Ellie took a deep breath. She hadn't expected the mood to shift in this direction, and she wasn't sure she could go along with it. She focused on driving instead. When she pulled into the driveway, Jordan asked,

"Are you okay? You've been quiet."

"I'm fine. Just tired."

So she'd noticed. Of course. There was no way Ellie could stall much longer, except...After they closed the front door behind them, Jordan pulled her close, kissing her deeply.

"How tired are you?" she whispered, the warm seductive tone almost enough to derail Ellie's plans. She was tempted, but there was a possibility she might hate herself the next morning, or whenever the secret came out. She couldn't take the chance that Jordan might hate her too for keeping this from her.

"Jordan. Let's sit down for a moment. We need to talk."

"Oh. Okay. I sense this might be uncomfortable," Jordan said as she sat at the kitchen counter. Ellie filled two glasses with water, taking a sip from one and setting the other in front of her fiancée. It was a pleasant thought. Jordan was right, though, the following conversation wouldn't be.

"I am so sorry."

"You changed your mind about the guest list? We need to come up with a final version soon."

"I know I shouldn't keep things from you, ever."

Jordan sighed. "I know Waters can be an ass. He's like that to everyone, and how he managed never to get fired is beyond me. I try to let you handle things your way, okay?"

"Yes, thank you, and you're right about everything, but…That's not it."

By now, Jordan had caught on her tone, knowing this was serious. There was alarm in her expression. Ellie wished she could ease her mind. Instead, she was going to do the opposite.

"Perhaps I don't want you to tell me. This evening was a surprise. I didn't expect a three-course homemade meal, and the volunteering."

"Jordan."

"Okay, out with it already."

"I didn't mean to snoop around, I swear. When I was in the bathroom, I knocked over a box by accident." She took another sip of her water. "There was pot in it. Not enough to sell, but…a stash. I am so sorry."

"Well, she did manage to cook, so at least she didn't get high today…"

That was not the reaction Ellie had expected.

"I feel terrible, but I thought you should know."

"Damn right I should know. Why didn't you tell me right away?" Jordan got to her feet, picking up the glass.

"I didn't want to make a scene. I thought we could talk this over here, and—"

"Damn her!" Jordan hurling the glass against the wall, where it shattered, was another reaction Ellie had not anticipated.

"Um, okay, let's take a deep breath. I know you're disappointed, and you have every right to be, but this is not the way. Please. Sit."

Jordan was already out of the room, and not much later, Ellie heard the front door, and then the sound of the engine.

Ellie stood, frozen, for a few seconds, but she never tolerated that kind of state for long. There was broken glass to clean up, figuratively and literally.

❦

"Jordan, hi. Did you forget something?"

Kathryn's PJs were a size or two too big, making her look frail. Jordan pushed that impression to the back of her mind, as she headed straight for the bathroom, finding the box immediately—its contents were still the same.

"What the hell is this?"

"What...how did you...Jordan, I swear this is not what it looks like."

"What does it look like? All this talk about being clean for years, it was a lie just like everything else. What were you thinking inviting cops into your house when you had this lying around?"

"Please, don't do this. I was so happy that you and Ellie came..."

"Oh spare me." The panic in Kathryn's voice was almost impossible to ignore, but Jordan couldn't alleviate any fears she might have, on the contrary. From the moment Ellie told her, her mind had gone on a one-way trip down memory lane, and it wasn't pretty. "It's still illegal, but frankly, it doesn't matter. This is it. I'm done. I can't do this anymore."

"Jordan, please wait!"

"No. I have no more patience for you and your lies."

"Would you let me explain?"

Jordan halted for a moment, already deeply ashamed of the way she'd left Ellie. She couldn't bring herself to regret a single thing she'd said to Kathryn. It was all true. This discovery brought back every single reason why life with Kathryn had made her feel trapped and unwanted at the same time, and why she was so much better off without her. Both Ellie and the well-meaning department shrink needed to understand that.

"There's nothing to explain. Forget what I said earlier, I don't want to see you or Jim at the wedding. You know what? You don't deserve to be there."

"You change your mind because of this? Are you sure it's a little bit of pot that you're worried about, or are you ashamed of your real parents?"

"Be careful what you say. My real parents are the people who gave me a home, and that will never change. I couldn't care less about how much money you have, or what you were going to wear, but this reminds me of every day of my life I hated because you and Jim were too stoned to give a damn."

Kathryn shook her head as she turned away. "That again. What do you want? How many times do I have to say I'm sorry until you understand—"

"No. No, it's you who doesn't understand. I wanted to kill myself because I thought no one could possibly love me. Guess what, I know better now. It took me a long time to understand where all of this was coming from."

"This is not fair. You can't blame me for every bad decision you made in your adult life!"

"Right. I don't blame you. I don't credit you for the good ones either, because you gave me nothing there. Don't bother calling me, ever again."

She yanked the door open to reveal a startled Ellie.

"I thought you might be here. Let me get you home?"

Jordan didn't give her an answer, just squeezed past her, and walked outside, taking a deep breath when the cool night air hit her face.

Ellie was struggling to keep up with her. "Wait. I mean it. I'm going to drive. I'm sorry it took me a moment, I...I wasn't sure what to do."

Jordan winced at the reminder of her earlier outburst. "That's okay. I got to say everything I wanted to say from the first moment she showed up. All that polite crap...I should have known better. What the hell is wrong with me? I shouldn't have fallen for any of it."

Ellie sat beside her in the driver's seat, silent.

"I'm so sorry." It occurred to Jordan that Kathryn had used the same words minutes ago. The realization felt damning.

Ellie stopped the car at the end of the narrow path and pulled her close. "It's okay. Whatever you need. I was so worried...I've never seen you like this."

If she said sorry often enough, would Ellie believe her?

⁂

The kitchen was spotless. Ellie, too, had needed some time to figure things out as it seemed. She was still here, so hopefully everything Jordan had said to Kathryn about her was still true too.

"You didn't have to do this."

"I know. And I know it's late, but can we talk?"

Jordan laughed self-consciously. "There's no way I can say no to you now, can I?"

"I'll seize the opportunity, then. I need to know we're on the same page. I suppose they're not invited now. I'm fine with that too. If a person keeps breaking promises, there should be consequences at some point."

"Yeah, maybe. I'm sorry. I know you were hoping it could work out differently...but you don't know her, not like I do. The two of them, though I can hardly blame Jim equally, knowing what I know now."

Ellie shook her head. "He decided to stay with her, so they were both responsible for you."

"She's right, too. I made a lot of bad decisions, and I can't blame all of them on her."

"Do you still want to get married?" Ellie asked softly.

"You don't?" The seconds ticked by in a moment of unadulterated fear.

"Of course I do. I don't want you to have to rush into something, because this is tearing you in every which direction. If it's all too much right now, with the house, and work, I can wait."

"No, it's all good. I want to. I've waited long enough for you."

Ellie's smile showed the same relief.

"Thank God. I already bought a couple of wedding magazines, and I've been fantasizing about bridal gowns."

"I'm good with that, and I swear, this was the last of the drama. I'll keep my distance from her from now on."

"You'll do what you have to do." Ellie took her hands on the table. "Let's just not break anything else, okay?"

"I promise. Not to change the subject, although, I'd like to. We glossed over it. You'll be all right with Waters?"

"Yes, absolutely. He can be a jerk, and I think he has a little too much sympathy for the wrong people, but I know it's only temporary. Carroll might partner me with Doss after, who knows."

"Yeah. The future's looking good, right?" Ellie was letting her off easily. Jordan would dwell a bit anyway, she knew from experience.

"It does."

"It's not just Kathryn who rattled me. I mean, that was obviously the main reason, but Derek and I closed this case, and it was awful. It caught me off guard, this guy, and the widow left behind. I wanted to give her a better reason than that he chose this."

"I know. But you can't find what's not there, and don't tell me you didn't look hard enough. I know you did."

"I passed it on to the folks in Fraud. I guess that was all. How about you? Any new suspects? Do you think someone's targeting homeless people?"

"My gut says yes, but I'm going to need a bit more. The only witness has a rap sheet of his own, domestic violence and carrying without a license, but he also has an alibi. And there's something I can't put my finger on—Potter was beaten up a few weeks ago by some guys who were wearing sweatshirts with logos. This could be anything. Businesses? No one knows."

"If it was local, he might have recognized them. It's pretty blatant for the perps to show up in identifiable clothing, unless there are many of those sweatshirts. Like..."

"A school!" Ellie finished the sentence for her. "Thank you so much! I love it when you're in my brain."

"Slow down," Jordan advised, though she was pleased and relieved to be back in safer territory. "It's still a needle in a haystack."

"Yeah, unfortunately, and that would mean neighborhood watch guy's alibi works out after all. Okay, but I'll look into that." She hid a yawn behind her hand. "Tomorrow. Well, later today. Let's go to bed now?"

Jordan didn't have any objections, though she lay awake for a long time, replaying the past few days in her mind, the Kenning case, Kathryn's promises and failure to keep them, her own reaction that had been far over the top. She recognized the pattern, of being truly happy and at the same time, terrified it could all be over in a heartbeat. She had to do better, she knew, trust herself, trust Ellie.

Bridal gowns. The prospect excited her in a way she had never imagined.

Ellie's lips were soft against her neck. "We're going to need so much coffee tomorrow."

"No kidding."

"You were right, you know. I wanted the happy ending so badly, for you, and selfishly, for me, too. I'm sorry it took me so long to understand that you were grieving too...for the parents you deserved to have right from the start."

Jordan turned around to pull her close. There were no more words necessary.

Chapter Seven

"What's this? You've been partying on a school night?"
Officer Casey Lyons asked, amused, as she perched
on the edge of Ellie's desk.

"Something like that," Ellie sighed. "Please tell me you have
something good."

"I do," Casey affirmed. "Ginny Collins. I talked to her at the
women's shelter. She's here and she wants to make a statement."

"Really?" This news gave Ellie the longed-for adrenaline jolt.
"I love you so much right now."

"I'll pretend I didn't hear that," Jordan, who walked by at an
untimely moment, said.

"I'll pretend she didn't say that," Casey muttered. "I don't
want to be uninvited. Interrogation 3."

"All right. And stop it with the silly jokes." Ellie didn't wait
for an answer, already on her way, eager to meet the witness that
might give her the big break for this case. As she stepped into
the room, Ellie was for a moment taken aback when she saw the
young woman. Ginny Collins looked like a teenager, cold and
scared.

"Ms. Collins, hi, I'm Detective Harding." She still had to
resist the urge to smile when saying this. "I have a few questions.
Would you like a coffee?" Might as well combine the practical
with the necessary.

"Do you have hot chocolate?" Ginny asked hopefully.

"I'll see what I can do. I'll be back in a minute."

Ellie's mind was reeling already as she headed to the break room, purchasing a coffee, a hot chocolate, a granola bar and a chocolate bar from the vending machine. If Ginny had the same concerns as Marco, how would they keep her safe as long as they only had a vague idea of the threat? She hoped this conversation would lead to something solid.

She returned to the room where Ginny was waiting for her, still shivering. Ellie kept the coffee for herself and set the other beverage and the bars in front of the woman who took it all in with a longing expression.

"Okay, let's start." At this moment, her cell phone rang. "Excuse me for a second."

On the other end was the last person Ellie had expected to call.

"Ellie, I know it's probably a bad time, but—"

"You're right, it is. I'm at work. Please, don't call this number again." Ellie pushed Kathryn and whatever motives she might have, out of her mind. "I'm sorry about that. Officer Lyons said you are concerned for your safety."

"I'm fucking scared, okay? They might come for us one by one. First Willie, now Lea...You gotta wonder who's next."

"Who are they?"

She shrugged. "Guys who hang out at the park, drunk, looking for a fight."

"Did you see any of them? Can you describe them?"

"I'm not sure. It was dark. I was scared."

"How old are you, Ginny?"

"What does that have to do with anything? I'm eighteen."

Ellie knew she couldn't let herself be distracted right now, even though the lack of options frustrated her. If Ginny told the truth and she was of age, she was too old for the foster system—then again, chances were that was where she came from.

"Are you taking this seriously? We are being attacked out there!"

"I am. I promise you. This is why whatever you can remember, is important. Take your time. I believe you, Ginny. We want to make sure it won't happen again."

"That's not what the other cop said."

"What cop?"

"The one Willie reported to. He said not to bother, that they can't do anything without a description."

Ellie found her to be sincere, and she was furious that someone on the job had brushed off a homeless man who'd been the victim of a crime.

"This is not right. I swear I'll look into this. Did you speak to anyone at the shelter, or anywhere else, who saw them?"

"They were harassing Meg, too, but I haven't seen her in a while."

"When was the last time you saw her?"

Ellie didn't want to scare her any more, but she didn't like what she was hearing.

"A couple of days ago. Wait...She called them frat boys. I don't know if that was for real, but they were about that age."

"That's very good. Do you have a place you can stay tonight?"

The young woman shrugged. "I guess."

"Great. Be careful, and if you remember anything else, please come by. I'll make sure that someone will take a message if I'm not here."

There was a knock on the door, and Casey Lyons peeked inside. "Ellie, the lieutenant wants to see you."

"I'll be right there." To Ginny, she said, "Could you please wait here for a moment?" Truth be told, Ellie wasn't sure if it was safe for her to go back out there. Perhaps this was a good opportunity to stall a little.

She hurried to get to Lieutenant Carroll's office, only to realize that Waters, Jordan and Derek were already there with their supervisor, all of them wearing serious expressions. For a brief moment, Ellie worried that she had done something wrong without knowing it, that she'd be off the case, or worse, fired—then she reminded herself that not everything was about her. She was right.

"The woman Officer Lyons brought from the shelter is still here?"

"Yes, sir."

"The shelter is burning as we speak. So far, one death, but several occupants have been injured. There's hardly any doubt anymore that someone is targeting the homeless community. Waters, Henderson, I want you at the scene, coordinate with Arson. Carpenter, you go to the hospital." Jordan nodded. "Harding, you'll join her after finding the woman a place to stay."

This was hardly a time to argue, so Ellie didn't, though she wondered why Carroll made Derek go with Waters instead of her.

"Sure. Yes, sir. Do we know who died?"

"Male, thirties, apparently he was doing janitorial work for the place."

"Okay. I'll be at the hospital," she said to Jordan, and their small group dispersed. Back in front of the room where Ginny had finished her treats, Ellie took a deep breath, wondering what to do next. Finding a place to stay for Ginny was easier said than done. The place where she'd come from was going down in flames, and someone out there wanted to kill her. They might have succeeded if Casey hadn't brought her here.

She had an idea and went to find Casey who was on her way out.

"Please, wait. You heard about the fire? I need to make arrangements for Ginny, but since she can't go back there, I'd like to put her in a motel. I want you to go with her."

"Okay, sure. Let me know when you're done."

Ellie finally stepped back into the room with Ginny.

"Slight change of plans," she said, trying to sound more optimistic than she felt. "I'd prefer if you didn't go back just yet. As I said, we are taking this seriously. Officer Lyons will take you someplace safe, and she'll stay with you."

"Please, find Meg," Ginny said. "I'm scared something might have happened to her."

Ellie didn't say what she was thinking—it was likely.

⚜

Ellie found Jordan with a woman who was about to go into surgery. She had broken her leg when she jumped out of a window in panic. Most of the patients had been admitted for smoke inhalation.

"Thank you. Get well soon." Jordan touched the woman's shoulder lightly before she turned to Ellie.

"I guess this confirms your theory."

"Yeah. Sometimes it sucks to be right. This was the only place for them to go, and now they barely escape with their lives. Did you find anything?"

"Nothing as to who set fire to the place, but there had been a sense of fear even before it happened. How's the university angle coming along?"

"It's coming along," Ellie answered. "Ginny told me earlier about a friend of hers who called the harassers frat boys. The thing is, now she's missing."

"I was going to talk to the woman who runs the place. She's here, wasn't injured, but she wants to make sure everyone has somewhere to go."

Ellie followed her along the hallway.

"You don't think it's odd that we're here together?"

"Why?"

"I don't know. It seems like a test. Maybe Carroll wants to know if we can work together?"

Jordan shook her head with a smile. "He already knows that. You were in the middle of an interview, and he needed a couple of detectives on the scene right away, that's all."

"Hm."

"It wasn't me either, I swear. I promised not to hover...anymore."

"Thank you. Let's do this, then."

The interviews confirmed that lately there had been a general air of unease and outright fear from the people coming to the shelter. The stories remained somewhat vague. A group of men looking to pick a fight.

"They are literally scared to death." Ellie sighed. "I don't believe it. If you're out there and trying to survive, you do pay attention to detail. It was unfortunate Willie Potter couldn't tell what was on that shirt, but everyone? How are we supposed to protect them if they don't trust us?"

Jordan looked thoughtful. "Unfortunately, many of them don't trust that we actually intend to protect them. Darla had some bad experiences with cops."

"Well, yeah, there are some people out there likely belonging to some organization, and they are worse. They are killing people at an alarming rate. Excuse me," she said when her cell phone rang. Ellie stepped aside, suppressing a curse when she saw the caller ID. She made a little more distance.

"I said I can't talk to you."

To her relief, Jordan had found Officers Lyons and Potts, and was talking to them.

"Please, don't hang up," Kathryn said urgently. "It's not about Jordan. There's someone here you should talk to."

"Why?"

"If you don't want to come, please send someone else. It's about the murders in the park. I swear I'm telling the truth."

"All right." Ellie looked over to where Jordan was still standing with the officers. She couldn't imagine how Kathryn could know anything about the case, but the status quo had her frustrated enough to acknowledge every possibility. She'd tell Jordan eventually, but now was not a good moment. "I'll be there as soon as I can."

"Thank you."

She disconnected the call and walked over to her colleagues. "Something came up, I need to leave," she said to Jordan who didn't question her. "I'll talk to you later."

"Sure."

It was odd, she reflected as she drove to Kathryn's home, how Jordan's biological mother was likely to become a witness again after leading them to an escaped felon before. Maybe she had changed—maybe this was her way of trying to redeem herself. However, Ellie could understand Jordan feeling betrayed. It wasn't the amount of pot Kathryn kept in her bathroom, but the fact that after all these years she still had a complicated relationship with the truth.

Kathryn stood in front of the trailer, arms crossed over her chest.

"Thank you for coming."

"You said you have information on the case?"

"Yes. Come in, please."

Ellie followed her into the confined space, startled to find a younger woman sitting at the table, her hands wrapped around a mug filled with steaming hot tea. She looked terrified.

"It's all right," Kathryn told her. "You can trust her. Ellie, meet Meg. She's been hiding from some people I think you'll want to take a closer look at."

⁕

The pieces were falling into place. Meg knew about members of a local fraternity that had beaten up Willie Potter. She had more to say about Lea's death, and she was scared for her own life.

"Could you identify any of them?" Ellie asked, feeling excited despite herself. A real lead. That could mean a sliver of hope for the people who had just lost a safe place. Justice for Willie and Lea. Proving Marco Raynor innocent. Was it possible that Kathryn could make all of this happen, the current conflict notwithstanding?

"I can give you names, but I need something in return. Kathy told me they torched the shelter. Those are killers. I can't ever go back to that park."

"I'll talk to the A.D.A. If you know something, Meg, you need to tell me. I spoke to Ginny earlier."

"She's okay?" Meg interrupted. "Thank God!"

"She's worried about you. If you help me now, we can put all of them away." Kathryn was leaning against the wall, observing them. Ellie hadn't missed the flash of doubt in her expression.

"I promise you."

"If they find out I told on them, they're going to kill me too."

"I'm not going to let that happen. I swear. Tell me what you know, and I will call the A.D.A. right away."

Meg sent an imploring look towards Kathryn who nodded. Strange to think that she seemed to be able to build such easy rapport with those young women, Meg, Darla's friend Serena she had hidden from a drug lord called Bud Ryder—but she couldn't seem to succeed with her own daughter.

"Okay then," Meg finally relented. "A group came to the park a few times. I think the university arranged it. They gave us addresses for where to get a warm meal or a place to stay the night, but also programs for jobs and school." She shrugged. "I guess it was their project. They were mostly nice, but this one guy...the way he looked at me, it scared me. Weeks later, he came back, and he brought some other friends, and instead of leaflets, they brought baseball bats. They killed Lea."

"Willie Potter's death wasn't ruled a homicide. How could that happen?" Ellie said more to herself.

"Someone didn't look hard enough?"

Ellie didn't like Kathryn's tone. She was hardly in any position to judge.

"Well, we don't know for sure yet. With Meg's help here, we will solve those cases. Let me make a call, and we can leave."

She caught A.D.A. Esposito right away and detailed the situation to her.

"Finally." Valerie sighed. "Bring her here right away. Anything that is moving this case forward. Is Carpenter anywhere near you?"

"No, not right now."

"All right, I'll call her. See you in a bit."

When she was done with the call, Ellie addressed the other women again.

"Okay, the A.D.A. is going to meet us right away. Let's go." When she turned to leave, Kathryn held her back. Ellie sensed that what she was about to say had to do with a private matter.

"Meg, could you please wait outside?"

Meg nodded and obediently left the trailer. Ellie stepped out of the somewhat desperate grip.

"Thank you, Kathryn. This is extremely helpful, but...I'm sorry. If you expected anything in return, I can't do that."

"Jordan is back to not talking to me, isn't she?"

"What did you expect? Look, this is her decision to make, but you should ask yourself, was there ever a time when she could rely on anything you said?"

"You weren't there."

"That is true, but I know from someone who was. I'm really sorry. I need to go back to work."

"Can't you tell her I'm sorry?"

"I can," Ellie said, thinking guiltily that for that to happen, she'd first have to tell Jordan about this meeting. "Thanks again. Please don't hesitate to call if there's anything else."

She walked away, with Meg in tow, lost in thought. Kathryn might have helped break the case. She was taking classes to learn to cook healthier, and she seemed to be taking in young women in danger on a somewhat regular basis. She wanted to be a presence in Jordan's life, but she still couldn't be a reliable one. Did good intentions count?

That was something only Jordan could decide.

※

Ellie conferred with Casey and let Meg and Ginny have a quick reunion. The two young women hugged, and Ginny tearfully thanked Ellie.

She set up a room for Meg and then found Waters and Esposito.

"That's your witness? You'll have to clean her up a whole lot before she gets anywhere near the stand." Ellie straightened her shoulders, willing not to take the bait.

"How do you know she's not on something?" Waters asked.

Meg had told her she didn't do drugs, and she'd sounded believable, as she had in every other part of her testimony. Kathryn sounded genuine, too, when she had them over for dinner, but Ellie didn't want to think about that now.

"She'll do fine, you'll see."

Waters and Esposito stayed outside while Ellie sat down with Meg once more, pointed out the cameras to her, and asked her to repeat, in as much detail possible, what she'd told Ellie earlier.

Meg didn't hold back.

"His name is Sean Norton. He came with a group from the university—they get extra credit for volunteer work, and some of them have developed a project to provide us with information. Short-term, a safe place to stay for the night, long-term, to get back on our feet." She shrugged. "He asked a lot of questions—and he got into an argument with Marco once. Most of them are cool, but Sean, he had no idea. I was wondering if he joined the project as some sort of compromise with the university."

"You saw this man several times, and he came back without the members of the group?"

"Yes. I don't know the others. A couple of them came only once or twice—I guess it wasn't for them after all. I recognized Sean, because he talked to me a lot, saying stuff like the streets are no place for a pretty girl. I heard about them roughing up Willie. Then, not long after that, Willie was dead. I was scared."

"I understand. Tell me about the night Lea died."

"I swear I didn't know at first that Marco got arrested. You know, Sean wasn't the only person causing trouble. There's this neighborhood watch wanting to clean up the park." Meg scoffed. "As if anyone feels safe if those guys run around parading their guns—but anyway, this one guy kept coming at Marco. He often drives his truck around the park in circles, to let us know he's watching. He did it that day, too…" She swallowed hard. "It got dark, and I didn't know where to go. I was already scared because of what happened to Willie. I wanted to talk to Marco and tell him to step back for a bit, because at the time, I thought those guys might be the more dangerous ones. Then I saw Sean…with the rock in the hand. There was blood on the rock, and his hand, and Lea…"

"You are absolutely sure it was him?"

"Yes. I was close enough to see his face. He looked right at me. That's when I freaked out and ran. A friend told me I could probably crash at Kathryn's for a couple of nights."

"Initially, you weren't going to come forward? What made you change your mind?"

"I was already feeling horrible, and many of us were afraid…Kathryn said to me I'd feel better if I told the truth, and that you could protect me. I hope that's true."

"You're talking about Kathryn Larson," Ellie made sure to confirm.

"That's right. I heard from another girl that I could go to her. She understands…She's been through a lot, and she came close to being homeless. Anyway, she called you, and that was it."

"Yeah." Ellie had to be careful not to lose her thread. It was odd and somewhat frustrating that Kathryn seemed to turn into a saint all of a sudden. How could people compartmentalize like that? How could she not take care of her own daughter? If that daughter had been anyone but Jordan, of course, Ellie would have given herself the answers easily. Drugs, loneliness, depression. And still.

"That was good advice, in any case. You've helped us a lot, and we'll make sure you're safe. I promise."

She had joined Esposito and Waters when after a knock on the door, Jordan came inside.

"I heard there's a new development in your case? I have good news too. A description of the arsonist's vehicle, including a license plate. Ron Heller. He's a student at the university."

"The plot thickens," Valerie said. "Sounds good to me so far. We'll go with Sean Norton first, and check Heller's alibi while you're there."

"You're ready to make an arrest?"

"Why are you surprised, Carpenter? You're not the only one around here who knows how to do their job."

Jordan didn't bother responding to Waters' comment.

"That's your witness?" she asked with a nod to Meg behind the glass.

"Yes. Look, Kathryn called me earlier. Meg was staying at her place, and Kathryn convinced her to talk to us. We have an ID, a witness to the crime."

"Okay. That doesn't sound too bad," Jordan said carefully.

"Even though she's your fiancée, you can give her a little more credit than that," Valerie chastised. "I, for one, am glad that we can move on from the neighborhood watch guy with domestic issues. I'll make sure you get your warrant."

"Ellie, can I talk to you for a moment?" Jordan asked.

Waters rolled his eyes, but there wasn't much he could say at the moment. They had to wait for Valerie anyway.

"I won't be far," Ellie told Waters, then she followed Jordan out of the observation area and into the hallway. When they were alone, she continued, "I'm really sorry. I had to check it out, and I had no idea what she was going to say would turn out to be this important. I swear I was going to tell you the first chance I got."

"And you did." To her surprise, Jordan pulled her into a quick, tight hug.

"You're not mad?"

"I knew Kathryn would try to draw you into this, and I know you can handle yourself. That she's being this do-gooder now, is new, and let me tell you, it's pretty confusing to me."

"I can imagine. She asked me to tell you she's sorry."

"I don't doubt that. I guess we have to postpone that conversation," she said when Waters and Esposito approached them.

"Come on, Harding," Waters said. "Let's find Norton. You want to go talk to Ron Heller?" he addressed Jordan.

"Sure. I'll get Derek, and we meet you there."

Chapter Eight

D erek was on the phone, lowering his voice when Jordan came to his desk. His behavior was sparking her curiosity. Besides, she'd prefer to occupy herself with someone else's affairs for a moment. Kathryn being the saving grace of a case once again? It bothered her. It probably shouldn't, as it had nothing to do with her biological mother's mistakes, or Jordan's present in which she was planning her wedding.

Ellie's case was moving forward—that was a good thing. Jordan was happy she had success early on, not that she'd ever doubted it.

"You're done? Come on, let's go to the university and speak to Heller now. Ellie and Waters will be there—turns out they found a good suspect this time. The murders, the fire...looks like it's all connected."

"Good news."

"Yeah, it is," she agreed.

Derek seemed happy—really happy. Jordan suspected it had more to do with the call than with the good news.

"I assume that wasn't work," she said, teasing, as they walked to the car.

"Assume all you want. I don't mind."

"Partners share, right? You're seeing someone?"

"No, I'm not. Stop it."

Jordan shrugged, ready to change the subject. "All right, it seems there is a connection between Heller and the murder suspect. Never mind the arson case is now homicide as well. With a little luck, we nail them both."

"Ellie's got a warrant?"

She nodded. "We can tie those guys together, we get our own soon enough."

"Let's do that then."

They didn't talk about anything but the case on the way, but when Derek started whistling, Jordan found her suspicions confirmed. She would find out, one way or another.

❧

After conferring with Ellie and Waters, they waited outside the lecture hall where Ron was sitting in a class. Having his classmates witness the police wanting to talk to him might jog something—if not the fact that Sean Norton, on the same baseball team and fraternity, was about to be arrested.

The door opened, and the students started streaming out. Ron came out of the hall with his arm around a blonde girl.

"Ron Heller?" Jordan identified herself and Derek. "We'd like to talk to you."

The girl's eyes widened.

"I'll see you later," he said to her, giving them a lazy smile. "Police? What did I do?"

"We were hoping you'd tell us. This is your car?" She related the license plate number, even though they already knew the answer.

"I assume you ran it already. I watch cop shows sometimes. The ones with the attractive chicks."

Jordan wasn't sure whether this was meant to be flattery or an insult. In any case she couldn't care less if he put her in either one of those categories.

"Well, then you can guess where this is going. We'd like you to come to the station with us. Talk in private."

To her surprise, he laughed.

"You know, I'd actually appreciate that. Less of an audience that way. I know you're not arresting me or anything, because you'd have shown me a warrant already—so I should call my lawyer, right?"

"Would that be your lawyer, or your daddy's?" Derek asked.

"What's it to you? Give me a minute to call him."

"Well, it's absolutely your right to call legal assistance," Jordan agreed. "You can do that at the station. In any case, it would help you if you're working with us."

"You're fishing. I gotta say, that's kind of hot."

It was Jordan's turn to laugh. "We can place your vehicle at the scene of a crime, and one of your classmates was just arrested. I'm not sure how hot you think that is."

He raised his eyebrows. "You're bluffing. Why would you arrest anyone?"

"We know that you and your friends tried to scare a number of homeless persons out of Patton Lake Park. Arguments, fights, a clever attorney will say it's one person's word against the other's, maybe get you off on a misdemeanor...murder is another story."

"Hey, careful there, okay? I didn't murder anyone."

"You know what? I believe you. But it's going to be a jury you'll need to convince."

"All right, you know what? This is ridiculous. I don't need a lawyer for this. I'll tell you what I know. Which isn't much, okay? You'll leave me alone after that?"

"If you didn't do anything wrong, why wouldn't we?"

Seeing his friend in handcuffs on the way to the interrogation room was good timing, Jordan thought. She shared a quick smile with Ellie before she and Derek sat down with Heller—he wasn't in handcuffs, but he looked less smug now.

"You can call your lawyer now, if you want."

"I don't need a lawyer. I didn't do anything illegal."

"So, for the record, you're waiving your right to an attorney?"

"Yeah, sure."

"Okay. Let's talk. Arson. Three people now dead including the man who died in the fire. That looks like a terrible strategy."

"There is no strategy. Yes, it was my car, but I lent it to somebody. I had no idea they were going to torch that place! You have to believe me."

Jordan perched on the edge of the table.

"Let's start at the beginning. Who borrowed your car for what purpose? You know Sean is doing his best to save his hide right now. It's now a matter of which one of you makes the smart decisions."

"It wasn't Sean. Jack is one of his buddies. He said he just wanted to run some errands."

"Jack hangs out in the park with Sean a lot?"

He looked uncertain, and for a brief moment, Jordan harbored the hope that this could be easy. Then he shook his head.

"I don't know anything about the murders, I swear. I heard them say they were annoyed with the bums at the park, but that's all. I didn't hear anyone say anything about killing them."

"Really. You know Sean was taking part in one of the university's programs, one that's supposed to help homeless people?"

"Well, yeah."

"You were in that program too? So you could choose your victims?"

"No. I mean, no, I wasn't in that program, and you got it all wrong."

"Do we? We have a witness that can identify Sean. She saw him with a rock in his hand, standing over the body. Were you there too? Did you guys have fun stabbing the woman, hunting her down—"

"No!"

"—finishing her off with that rock?"

"Stop it! I want my lawyer now."

"I'll give you five minutes. You can either tell us the truth or call your lawyer after that."

Exasperated, she left the room, Derek following her.

"That was borderline," he remarked.

"Yes." She sighed. "Almost got him. Let's see what's going on next door."

Valerie Esposito was in the observation area with Ellie. On the other side of the glass, Sean Norton sat up straight in his chair, his expression unreadable.

"They're not talking," Valerie summed up the situation.

"Not yet. For guys like that, it's always about ego," Jordan said. "Heller knows something. And he's not so cocky anymore."

"Ego, huh?" Ellie turned to the two-way mirror. "This one is not just cocky, he's outright creepy. We might have to bring in the other kids from the program, see if they noticed anything...Wait. I have an idea." She went back into the room and sat across from Norton.

There was a minute change to his demeanor, his expression reflecting arrogance. He was trying to test her, but Jordan had seen perps underestimate Ellie before.

They usually regretted it.

"So...it seems your buddy Ron is supplying my colleagues with interesting information."

He scoffed. "I don't believe it."

"If he keeps talking, it won't matter what you believe. We already have a credible witness, and Ron is backing them up. So far, no surprise. What surprises me is that it was him, not you, who came up with the idea."

"What?"

Sean Norton started laughing. "He said that?"

"Aren't you glad? That means he'll be the one doing time. I guess if he's the one who's tough enough to kill people, he can handle prison."

"Who says I couldn't?" he asked, sounding irritated.

"Ron, for one, says that. I'm beginning to think he's right. I mean you have the chance here to tell us what was really going on, and so far, I don't see you making use of it. Not very smart if I—"

"Shut the fuck up!"

He hadn't said it that loudly, but the menacing tone was unmistakable. Ellie, to her credit, didn't even shrink back.

"Excuse me?"

"You think this is just about those hobos, think again. Some people need to be taught a lesson, and the fucking police aren't doing it."

"You are?"

"They are garbage," he spat. Now Ellie flinched. Jordan did too, like every decent human being would have.

"They are people. Human beings who are a lot stronger than you are."

He shook his head, amused. "Lady, slap a Band-Aid on that bleeding heart of yours and wise up. This is my advice to you, by the way. Be glad that someone's doing the job for you."

"You want to give me advice? Then help me understand. Why Lea? Why set the shelter on fire—if you don't want to see them, why destroy a place that helps homeless people?"

He shrugged. "I wouldn't expect you to understand it. The fire—that was Ron's idea. To me, it doesn't quite do the trick. As for the old hag, she was the perfect subject."

Ellie leaned a tad closer. "Perfect for what, Sean?"

He smiled at her. "I wanted to see someone die. Know what it's like."

Ellie kept her expression neutral, even though Jordan was sure she felt as sick as she did, and everyone with her in the room.

"I see. You've helped me a lot indeed." She pushed her chair back and came to join her colleagues outside.

"I guess that will do it. Damn, there's an ugly side to humanity."

"No doubt. You did a great job though," Jordan hurried to say, aware of Valerie's amused expression. "It's going to make mine a lot easier. I'll go finish up with Ron now."

Ellie beamed at the praise, though she still looked pale.

"This is good, right?"

"Beginner's luck," Waters commented. "Don't expect it to be always this easy." Behind his back, Jordan rolled her eyes and then made her exit.

⁘

Today wasn't the first time Ellie had looked into the abyss of a killer's mind. This time, she hadn't been in danger, but Sean Norton's words stayed with her regardless during the rest of the day. People like him presented a dire reminder that prevention and education, while essential, could only go so far with a certain percentage of the population.

83

"There I thought Stanton was an asshole, but apparently, there's no bottom where that is concerned."

"You're figuring that out only now, Harding? I seem to remember your girlfriend was kidnapped by a serial killer."

While she didn't appreciate the reminder, Ellie had to admit Waters had a point.

"Let's just say I'm glad we caught him."

"Well, that was the fun part. I don't know if you still feel lucky when you see the files we have to go through next."

Ellie couldn't help thinking about what would happen to Meg and Ginny in the long run, while she had the luxury of moving on to another case.

***

She met Jordan at the car after her shift. Ellie got in and sighed.

"You're not still feeling sick?" Jordan asked, leaning over for a brief moment to kiss her softly, before she started the engine. "I was hoping for a celebratory drink."

"People like that will always make me sick, but sure. There's somewhere I'd like to go first, if you don't mind."

"No problem. Where are we going?"

Jordan's expression revealed her surprise, but she didn't comment when Ellie gave her directions to the cemetery.

"I'm sorry if this looks like a bizarre way of introducing you to my parents, now that we're going to get married. I don't mean it that way. I just felt like dropping by."

"I understand. It's a big day. I wish I could have met them."

"Yeah. They would have loved you. I...I've been going more lately, but I have to admit I didn't for a while. Almost the whole time we've been together."

"Why?" Jordan asked. There was no judgment in her tone, just curiosity.

"I don't know. I guess I felt like I had to prove something to myself, have something to show for, especially after the attack. Now...I have a whole lot, a promotion and an engagement ring. Surprise, no matter how much I achieve, it still doesn't bring them back."

Jordan took her hand at a red light, and Ellie let herself be comforted by the warmth of the touch.

"I'm sorry. I didn't mean to get all dramatic." In fact, she hadn't said these things out loud to anyone. With Jordan, she could. It was a relief to know.

"That's okay. Would you like to get flowers?"

"I didn't think about...maybe. Yes."

They stopped at a flower shop where Ellie had the florist put together a bouquet of spring flowers.

When they arrived at her parents' plot, there was already a bouquet of long-stemmed roses draped across the grave.

"What the—" At the last moment, she reminded herself of the place they were at. "Okay, they are nice, but this is weird."

Jordan waited patiently.

"No one comes here except me—ever."

"Maybe someone wanted to be friendly."

"These are expensive. Unless my parents had some rich friends I don't know about...I doubt someone would do this as a random kind gesture."

Maybe she was still freaked out by the idea that somebody wanted to kill just to see what it was like...maybe some people were kind. Truth be told, Ellie hadn't made much of an effort to keep in touch with friends of her parents. The depth of loss couldn't compare, at least that's how she had felt at the time. Perhaps she should find some of them, see if they wanted to talk some time.

"On the other hand, you could be right. There are a few people I should probably call at some point. It took me a long time, but...I knew they would want to talk about Mom and Dad, and at the time, I couldn't."

Jordan nodded. "I know it's not the same, because my parents were alive all along, but I understand you get used to burying it."

Ellie stared at the roses for a long moment.

"Maybe. I shouldn't have. They were good people. And they had some good people in their lives that cared about them, that I shut out. You had every reason to feel about Kathryn and Jim the way you did..."

"Yeah. Her recent Samaritan deeds notwithstanding. Are you really worried about those flowers?"

"I'm not sure. I'll see if there are others and perhaps make a few of those calls finally."

Ellie knelt down to put her bouquet next to the roses.

When she got up, Jordan pulled her into an embrace. "Thank you for taking me here," she said.

"I'm not sure what to say to that, but I think it's time for that drink now. Let's go."

❧

Cliff Waters wasn't at the *Night Shift*, but Derek sat at a table with Detective Maria Doss, making Jordan wonder if they had rekindled their brief relationship—though the setting didn't look terribly intimate. In any case she was glad she and Ellie could invite them both to the wedding without worrying.

"Hey, Harding, good work," Doss greeted Ellie. "Are you guys worried about your record yet?"

The latter part was meant for Derek and Jordan. She shrugged.

"Wait, you hold a record?" Ellie asked, her eyes wide. "How come no one ever told me?"

"You've only been around us for a few days, have a little patience," Doss advised. She gave Jordan a quizzical look. "How are you not exhausted? No offense, Ellie. You're the reason I can work solo now, for the first time in years, and I'm loving it. Now, let's talk about people that aren't solo. Are you all ready for the big day?"

Jordan shared a look with Ellie, certain that she was thinking the same thing. *Basically, we need to take care of everything yesterday—this weekend, to be realistic.*

"Sure, it's going great," she said, eliciting a smile from Ellie. "No one's got any allergies, right?"

At this moment, Ellie looked downright panicked.

"Relax! Everyone came to Marcus' retirement party, and nothing bad happened, remember? People were all right with what Maria served at her birthday too."

"Well, I don't think I ever met a cop with a donut allergy," a cheery voice said, making them all turn around.

"Hey guys. I hear there's a wedding to plan, and correct me if I'm wrong, but I think the maid of honor hasn't been announced yet."

"Kate, hi. I hope that means you're volunteering? It's all hands on deck."

Kate pulled herself a chair and sat down, placing her glass on the table.

"I'll definitely be here for a while. I've finally decided to go back to school next semester. I'll be working for friends of my grandparents over the summer, but that leaves me plenty of time to see off my best friend into marriage." She only gave a quick glance to Derek who smiled as if none of this was news to him—Jordan concluded that in all likelihood, it wasn't.

Ellie leaned over to hug her. "I'm so glad you're here."

It wasn't self-evident, after Kate had lost her fiancé shortly before the planned wedding. However, it seemed that she was happy with her decisions.

Jordan wondered if she could stick with her decision to never talk to Kathryn again, or if she'd been out of line, with her, with Ellie.

"Me too," Kate said, stealing another quick glance. "So, tell me, what are you going to wear? What's the menu? Who's coming?"

Maria laughed. "Don't scare them."

"I'm not scared," Ellie said. "However, we're going to be very busy in the next few weeks."

Chapter Nine

E llie's emotions were all over the place on this day, and she was grateful Jordan was able to simply go along with it when she was in this kind of mood. Okay, so her mixed emotions came with pleasant results for her soon to be wife. It was incredibly liberating to close the door of their own home behind them and leave a trail of clothes all over the floor, knowing there'd be no one to walk in on them.

Eventually, they made it to the bedroom, but not before spending some time on the new couch.

Her mind clear again, Ellie gathered magazines and invitation samples and spread them all over the bed.

"Big day," Jordan commented. She sat back against the headboard, now wearing a tank top and shorts, her cheeks still flushed. Ellie was tempted, but she wanted to finalize one more thing today.

"Yeah. And I got reminded of everything we haven't gotten done yet. So, how about this one?" She held up one of the samples. "It's simple and classy, and I think they can do it rather quickly."

"That's a good idea."

"It's a good thing the people we want there will RSVP in person, so we can go to the caterer right away and tell them how much food we need. I believe Kate and Derek might come together."

"Yeah, given that they left together earlier, it's a safe bet."

"You think Maria will have a plus one?"

Jordan shrugged. "No idea."

"You think I should ask Cliff? I'm not sure he even cares, but I guess it would be odd not to ask him."

"Ask him. I don't think there's a chance in hell he would want to be seen at a lesbian wedding."

Ellie had to admit that it was a possibility. "Libby, Casey, Wes," she said the names out loud while writing them down. "You're sure about Kathryn and Jim? I don't mind either way, and I'm sure neither do Jack and Pauline."

"I'm sure," Jordan said, and her tone left no doubt that the subject was closed for her.

"Okay. There's someone I'd like to call, a couple of friends of my mom she was close with. I haven't talked to them in years, and I don't even know if they want to talk to me, but I want to give it a try. Darla. Oh. The lieutenant? What's the etiquette for that? Sergeant Bristol might want to come. If we invite Cliff, then he should be on the list too. I really owe him for letting me work with you guys so often. Valerie?"

"Um. I don't think so. And I don't think she'll feel left out. Don't say it."

"I wasn't going to. No exes, I'm totally fine with that."

Jordan laughed. "I'm so relieved. Seriously, I think we should keep it down to a comfortable number. Everyone gets along."

"That's the plan."

<hr>

It wasn't until the next evening that Ellie found the time and the courage to make the call. She didn't have a recent phone number, so after her shift, she sat in her car and did a quick internet search on her phone. Jordan was working late. They'd meet at home after.

No more delays.

Ellie found a social media account, and from there it didn't take her many detective skills to come up with a phone number. She thought she might not even recognize the voice, but when the phone was answered, and Madeline Kaplan spoke, her throat went tight. The last time they'd talked, it had been at the funeral. Ellie had barely been able to acknowledge anyone on that day. All she knew was that she felt all alone in the world, no matter how many people were present.

Everything had changed. She was planning her wedding.

"Hello? Who is this?"

She cleared her throat, realizing that she'd been lost in thought.

"Madeline? It's Ellie Harding." A few seconds ticked by, and Ellie hurried to fill the silence. "You probably think I'm out of line, calling you after all those years. I'm really sorry I never reached out before. It was just…It seemed too hard. I'm sorry I didn't realize it was hard for you too."

"Ellie, hold on, I'm so glad to hear from you! How are you?" Madeline's voice sounded shaky, and Ellie was afraid they might both be crying by the end of the call.

"Much better than when you saw me the last time. I'm doing well," she said. "This is part of why I called. I was wondering if you'd like to have a coffee sometime."

"I'd love to," Madeline said without hesitation. "I've felt bad, too. I thought I maybe should have tried harder—but you made it pretty clear that you didn't want the contact with your parents' friends. May I ask you what made you change your mind?"

Ellie sighed. "I realized that even if I don't talk about them, I still think about them every day. I thought I couldn't bear to hear the stories, about everything you shared, but the truth is I want to know. It's even more important to me now because I'm getting married."

"Ellie, honey, that's fantastic! I'd love to hear all about it. Why don't you come by for dinner tonight? And bring your partner. We have so much catching up to do, why not start as soon as possible?"

"I...I can ask. Are you sure it's okay?"

Madeline laughed. "I'm cooking for half a dozen people anyway, what's two more? Come. You remember my family, right? Susie has her own business now. Walt is away in college, and the twins are growing up too fast."

Ellie had vague memories of Madeline's children.

"Wow," was all she could say. "You must be so proud."

"I am. I can't wait to see you, and I'm happy to answer any questions you might have."

Was it too fast, too easy? Ellie wondered. But why shouldn't it be easy for once?

"Thank you so much. Just one more thing—I don't mind, but I was wondering if you left flowers on the grave recently? Long-stemmed roses?"

"I'm afraid that wasn't me. Of course, Meri and Pat would be worth it, but I don't believe there's actually anything there...the soul, you know?"

"I understand. Thanks. I'll see you later," Ellie said and ended the call. Meri and Pat. Now her eyes were welling up, but she didn't have a lot of time to indulge in the emotion. Her next call was to Jordan.

"Change of plans, if you don't mind," she said. "I called Madeline, my mom's BFF? She was so happy about the call she invited us to dinner. Tonight."

"Are you okay? You don't sound happy." Jordan didn't waste any time.

"I'm good, just a little...shaken, I guess. This is a bit more intense than I thought, but I said I'd come. You think you can make it?"

"Looks like it. Nothing that can't wait until tomorrow, frankly. Does she know your fiancée is a woman?"

Ellie understood the real question, *does she care?*

"She said 'partner' but I'm not sure how she meant it. In any case, I don't think it's a problem. I can't remember my parents hanging out with that kind of people."

"I just want you to be okay. All right. I'll sneak out as soon as I can."

"How about now? I'm still in the parking lot."

Jordan laughed. "That would work, too."

Things were going well for Ellie, so it was probably time to stop worrying, Jordan reflected as they arrived at the address Madeline Kaplan had given Ellie.

She had done well on her first case, her best friend was back in town to be her maid of honor, and she had reconnected with a friend of her parents', all in a matter of days. Ellie never hesitated when it came to the important things in life, and she'd rather worry about it later than miss a chance. Jordan had to remember that. She had to remember that not everyone's parents, and their friends, were irresponsible and unreliable.

Still, she was nervous when Ellie rang the doorbell. She'd had girlfriends before who weren't out to their family or where the introduction to the parents turned awkward. Bethany had been in the latter category, though they hardly ever saw her parents. It didn't matter at the time.

It mattered now, because Kaplan was the closest connection Ellie had to her parents, especially her mother.

A girl of pre-teen age opened the door to them, regarding them curiously.

"Hi," she said, and into the slightly awkward silence, "I'm Sarah."

"Hi Sarah. I'm Ellie, and this is Jordan. Your mom..."

"Sarah, did you answer the door? Ellie. Oh my God. You're all grown up." She wrapped Ellie into a tight hug before shaking Jordan's hand.

"It's so nice to meet you too. This day is just full of wonderful surprises. Come on in."

Jordan caught Ellie's smile to her. She, of course, had been right about the kind of people her parents were friends with. Madeline Kaplan seemed genuine. Why shouldn't she be?

Ellie was easy to love.

After dinner, Susie Kaplan and her husband said goodbye, and the twin girls, Sarah and Lily, went to do their homework. Jordan and Ellie sat in the den with Madeline and her husband Brad. They had taken out various photo albums, and a bottle of Scotch. Jordan declined the latter, as she was the one driving.

She excused herself as her cell phone rang, thinking Ellie looked a bit overwhelmed. Perhaps it was time to call it a night soon.

"Carpenter." She had stepped aside into the kitchen area, from which she still had a good view of the scenery.

"It's April. You asked me to look into Andrews Secure Living? I'm not sure this has anything to do with the case you closed, but there's definitely something shady going on."

Jordan instantly switched from monitoring the cozy reunion scene to shop talk with the detective she'd asked for a favor. Since she hadn't heard anything from April in a few days, she had assumed there was nothing.

"Can I meet you tomorrow, first thing in the morning?"

"Will you buy me a coffee? Then we have a date."

"You people in Fraud drive a hard bargain. Okay, sure. I'm curious."

"You won't be disappointed. I'll see you there," April promised.

"Thanks. Bye."

That was good news indeed. No proof in the world would bring her husband back, but knowing she'd been right might help Mrs. Kenning after all.

She joined Ellie and their hosts, apologizing once more.

"Oh, I'm sure it was important," Madeline said. "You two are doing such amazing work. Ellie's mom and dad would be beside themselves with pride if they were here now."

"I don't doubt that. I'm very proud of her. Did Ellie tell you that she just solved her first big case?"

Ellie gave her a grateful smile. No matter how important it was to confront your past, sometimes it was helpful to remind yourself of adult achievements. Jordan could relate to that more than anyone.

Ellie was barely waking up when Jordan came out of the shower the next morning.

"I thought you had a little more time," she said, sounding disappointed.

"I wish. I promised April to buy her a coffee."

"Okay, go on. Who's April?" She sat up, leaning against the headboard.

Jordan was pretty sure she was only teasing—but in her opinion, it was too early in the morning for that. "April from Fraud, regarding the Kenning case?"

Ellie sat up straighter. "Really? I thought that was closed?"

"It is. Just something I asked her to look into it. That company really worked hard to badmouth the poor woman and her husband."

That prompted Ellie to get out of bed and fold her into a hug. "What's that for?"

"You're a good person. And I love you."

"I love you too. I'm not so sure about the other thing."

"You're still thinking about Kathryn?" Ellie asked softly.

Jordan sighed. "It shouldn't be such a big deal, right? I try to be consistent, so I don't invite her. On the other hand, it would only be a few hours."

"Some of the most important hours in our lives."

"Yeah, but shouldn't I be the bigger person in this? The grown-up?"

"Kathryn should have been the grown-up a long time ago, but she wasn't. She's helped with two rather big cases, and she opened her home to Serena and Meg even knowing it could put her in danger. Is that enough? I'm not sure if it would be for me."

"I'll give that some thought. What about you? You're still okay with how everything went yesterday?"

"It was a bit quick," Ellie admitted. "But yes, I'm okay. All right. I guess you need to get going. Is she cute?"

A non-committal sound was all the comment Jordan was willing to give.

"Hey, Harding, there's someone here to see you," Doss told her as she was passing her by in the hallway. Curious, Ellie went to see Marco Raynor waiting by her desk.

"Mr. Raynor, it's good to see you."

"I'm surprised I'm saying this to a cop, but I'm glad to see you too. I wanted to thank you for catching Lea's killer."

"That's my job."

He shrugged. "I didn't think anyone would give a damn."

"Well, it's a good thing you were wrong." Ellie noticed he was fidgeting. "Is there anything else you'd like to talk about?"

"No, it's all right."

"Are you sure? In any case, if there's ever a problem, please let me know."

He folded the card she gave him and put it into the pocket of his jeans.

"What are you going to do?"

"Oh, I actually might have a job lined up. People at the university were shocked that some of their own students were killers. They stepped up the program."

"That's good news. Best of luck to you."

"Thanks, Detective. Have a good day."

Ellie watched him walk away, wondering if she'd ever see him again. Something was nagging at the back of her mind. No reason, right? Perhaps she was just nervous because the big day was arriving rapidly. Meanwhile, she had a job to do.

⁂

April had already a tall latte in front of her when Jordan arrived at the café across from the station.

"Good morning. I'm sorry, I couldn't wait. This might be the only good kind of caffeine I get today."

"No problem. This is it?"

April handed her the thin blue folder. "Pretty dubious business practices. We are looking further into that. I know you'd like to give the widow some piece of mind, but I want you to be vague about what you share with her. There's still a chance we might get those sons of bitches."

"Sounds good to me."

Jordan ordered a black coffee and asked the waitress for the check. She opened the folder and began to skim the pages, evidence detailing on how employees were pressured to push products on clients, punished if they didn't make the quota.

"Wait until you get to the end," April said. "It's some messed up stuff, but we have to tread carefully. People are afraid for their jobs, here, and in companies they partnered with."

"Anyone afraid for their lives?"

"I'd say that's a matter of interpretation so far. In any case, the climate must have been pretty horrible."

"Thanks."

"Any time. And by the way, congratulations on the wedding."

Jordan's surprise must have shown. April laughed. "Word gets around quickly. It's not the first lesbian wedding in the department, but you know how it is. We are always interested in what's going on in Homicide."

"I guess."

"In any case, the more of us, the better. Thanks for the coffee. I hope you'll find what you're looking for in those reports."

"I'm sure I will."

◦◦◦

Jordan spent her lunch break reading over the materials, finding confirmation of what April told her. That meant the death of Daniel Kenning had been a suicide. The circumstances were obvious, but there wasn't enough evidence to suggest a homicide. The least she could do was to give Mrs. Kenning her final conclusion. She already knew that the medical examiner had ruled his death a suicide—what April had given to Jordan showed that Mrs. Kenning hadn't been crazy to think the company had put a lot of pressure on all employees.

Fifteen minutes after her shift, Jordan knocked on the woman's door.

"Can I come in for a moment? I promise I won't bother you for long."

Mrs. Kenning shrugged. She didn't seem to have a strong opinion one way or another.

"I already know there's nothing you can do. Unless that changed, I'm not sure why you're here."

"We are sure that your husband took his own life," Jordan said. "I'm so sorry. Even if it wasn't a homicide, it doesn't mean you were completely off. It's out of my hands now, but it seems there is a culture of harassment and threats at your husband's firm. I promise you that someone will look into that."

It wasn't much, she knew. It wouldn't bring a grieving widow her husband back.

"You know, it's strange, right, that some days, I'm mad at him before anything else. He left me alone to deal with all of this! We could have worked it out somehow."

"He didn't mean to hurt you. In a moment like that, people can't see any way out."

Mrs. Kenning straightened her shoulders. "I know that too. Thank you, Detective. I'm relieved to know someone believes me. Maybe the emails will stop, too."

"What emails are you talking about?"

"They come every day. I don't recognize the sender, but I have an idea—they want to get back at me for talking to the police, scare me. I've lost everything," she said, sounding desperate. "What the hell do they think I'm afraid of?"

"Show me," Jordan said. "I swear we're going to do something about that too."

After reading over the three emails in Mrs. Kenning's inbox, she excused herself and called April.

"Hey. I have something you should take a look at. There might be harassment charges to add to your list."

"I like this collaboration already." April laughed. "I'll pay for the coffee next time. Send it over."

Chapter Ten

U nlocking the door to her home half an hour later, Jordan was surprised to hear laughter from the living area. She walked in on a cozy scene. Ellie and Kate were hunched over the bridal magazines, prompting Derek to say, "I'm so out of here." No one took him seriously, and he looked quite comfortable with his beer in hand.

Darla sat next to them, her son Avery playing with blocks on the carpet.

Ellie all but jumped to her feet and greeted her with a kiss.

"You're home! I would have warned you about all this, but I don't think you read any of your messages."

"It's fine. Who's cooking?"

"*Giacomo*. They should be here in about ten minutes."

"I love you," Jordan said with emphasis, before she went to the fridge to get a beer for herself. She was still switching from work mode to evening with friends, flashes of earlier conversations vivid.

"Hey."

Darla had joined her in the kitchen area while keeping an eye on her son. "Things are going pretty well for you two, I see."

"Yes, they are." Jordan opened her beer, leaning back against the counter, finally relaxing. Once the sender of the emails was identified, it would probably help April's case. Give Mrs. Kenning further closure. Things were good.

"You know I still keep in touch with Serena?"

"How is she?"

"Doing okay. She found a job, and she's going to this new place where you can help out and get meals. They teach you how to cook, too."

"Is there something you want to tell me?" Jordan winced as her words came out a bit harsher than she'd intended them. "I'm sorry. Long day."

"It's okay, but wow, I can't get anything past you, can I?"

"I'm a detective, remember?"

"All I meant to say was I can imagine it's difficult. Serena and Kathryn talk...So I got a little bit of both sides."

"You don't really know both sides," Jordan said, taking a sip from her bottle. "Let's not talk about this."

She was literally saved by the bell. She'd give the delivery person an extra tip for good timing.

⚯

"It's not like I have a problem with them per se, but where is it going to end? People marrying their brother or sister because they feel like they have the right to do so?"

On the other side of the door left ajar, Ellie curled her fingers into a fist so hard her fingernails were biting into the skin of her palm. She was counting to ten. She knew that the majority of people in general, and in her workplace, were better educated and more decent than that. She also knew that exceptions were everywhere, and Chris Atwood had been on that list since he called Kate a slut for daring to move on with her life after a horrible loss. Waters, who seemed to be friendly with Atwood, was another one to watch. His casual sexism came as no surprise.

She had seen him acting that way with Doss a few times, making her glad that his retirement was near.

Sadly, age wasn't the only factor. Ellie was troubled to think that someone of her own generation, even younger, could have such a closed mind, but here it was.

"Well, things are moving into a different direction now," Waters answered.

"Yeah, thank God. No more special rights for everyone who cries discrimination. It's been overdue."

Ellie cleared her throat and pushed the door open. The two men barely noticed her as she walked in. On the bright side, they were alone. It didn't seem like there were many more colleagues involved in this kind of gossip.

"Remember those files you wanted me to go through? I think I found something," she said.

Neither of them was the slightest bit self-conscious regarding the conversation she'd just overheard. Ellie hadn't expected it either.

Waters picked up his coffee. "All right. What do you have?"

She had spent a day and a half over dusty files concerning a drug dealer who had dropped off the face of the earth after getting out on bail, charged in the recent murder of a young waitress. Waters had opened this case before her promotion. The dealer's ex-girlfriend had been interviewed but swore she didn't know where he was. Silence on the streets as well.

Ellie had gone over a pile of court transcripts and interviews per Waters' request, in the search for something, anything anyone might have overlooked.

"What about the girlfriend's sister?"

"What about her?"

Atwood rolled his eyes and left.

Ellie opened the file she was carrying to a page she'd marked with a sticky note. "I see here that Ashley, the girlfriend, has a sister."

"Yeah, I remember her sitting in the courtroom."

"Ashley isn't talking to the police, but maybe her sister will. She might know something about Ashley's relationship with Lemont that could help us."

"It's a long shot," he said. Ellie sensed that the lack of progress in this investigation might make him go for it.

"I could go right now and talk to her, so we can check that off the list?"

"All right. You do that."

So much for live and learn...but at least she'd be able to escape the files. Ellie sneezed three times as she left the building. Dust, that was all there was to it. She couldn't afford to get sick weeks before her wedding. No way.

❦

Ashley's sister Jayne lived in an apartment complex, with a small playground in the back that looked old and rundown, more of a safety hazard than a place to let children play. She reluctantly let Ellie in.

"I don't know why you keep bothering Ashley," she said. "Please don't take it personally. I just don't see the sense in it. Ryan Lemont being out of her life was the best thing that ever happened to her. She sure as hell doesn't miss him."

"Your sister told us she doesn't know where he is."

"Then it's the truth. That's all I can tell you."

Ellie couldn't yet figure out if her defensive demeanor meant that she was annoyed by the police's repeat visits, or if she was hiding something. In any case, she planned to find out.

"You have a pretty good idea of what Ashley and Ryan's relationship was like."

Jayne scoffed. "You bet."

"Do you think it's possible he threatened her?"

"Only all the time? But I don't think he's been around in a while, if that's what you're asking. She would tell me."

"If he shows up, it's important that you tell us."

"Yeah, we've heard that before. I believe he moved on. Things got too hot around here. I guess he thought that this time, you actually have something on him, so he split. As I've said, for me and Ashley it's only a good thing."

Ellie took her time to consider the implications of her words. "Did he ever threaten you?"

"Only when I told Ash to get the hell away from him. Regardless, I don't want that kind of people around my kids."

"I understand. Just let me know if anything changes."

Jayne took the card from her, regarding it thoughtfully.

"You know, I don't like these types that love to parade their guns and claim to clean up the neighborhood...except lately, it seems to have worked around here. Ryan took off, and I think a few others are gone too. So that's not a bad thing...right?"

"These types...Is there anyone in particular?" Ellie thought that this kind of job was best left to the police, but she didn't share her assessment with the woman now that she got her to open up a bit.

"I don't know their names. Big guy in a truck, and a few others."

"That's all right. Please call me if you hear from Mr. Lemont."

She had to admit, later when she brought her meager findings to Waters, that the long shot hadn't panned out the way she hoped it would.

"It was worth checking," he said to her surprise. "Back to the drawing board."

"I wonder if it's a coincidence that she mentioned the neighborhood watch."

"Yeah, let go of that already. These guys aren't doing anything illegal, and you don't want a lawsuit a few weeks into your new job."

While she hadn't forgotten about his approval of Atwood's stereotypes, Ellie had to admit he wasn't too far off. She had to be careful—nevertheless she was curious about the hold this neighborhood watch seemed to have in certain areas.

When she looked up, she saw the lieutenant heading their way. His expression was serious, his tone curt and clipped when he spoke.

"Hikers found a body near Patton Lake Park. Please tell me you got the right guys the first time."

"Sir, there's no doubt that—"

"Save it, Harding. We'll sort this out later. Go and find out what the hell happened."

⁓⁓

Ellie was lost in thought on the way to the park, and Waters didn't offer anything to ease her mind. Was it possible? They had witnesses, confessions, DNA all lined up. A man had sat across from her and detailed how much he enjoyed killing homeless people. His deep and disturbing disdain had almost made her sick. A friend of his had set fire to a shelter to "send a message."

She hadn't made a mistake.

But if that was true, there was an even more disturbing possibility: Another killer. At least she had gradually followed the advice of her colleagues and donned some more practical clothes.

The sky had been clear this morning, but now a constant drizzle was coming down. Thank God for small favors, like a coat with a hood.

Ellie's day went downhill from there.

They arrived at the scene where unis had already taped off the area, onlookers surrounding it even in the bad weather. It was like an uncanny déja-vu that only got worse when she got to look at the body.

"Single GSW from what we can determine at the moment. Bullet's still inside. I'll be able to tell you more after the autopsy."

Dr. Adams' voice came as if from far away. Ellie's hand went to her mouth.

The victim was Marco Raynor.

The hits kept on coming. Ellie had been excited about the notion that solving the case would bring justice to the victims. Lea. Willie Potter, who, even if the medical examiner's ruling still held, had been brutalized before. The janitor who had died in the fire, and the women who had lost the shelter. She had hoped that closing the case also might lead to new options for some of the people she'd met along the way, including Marco Raynor. Whatever new path he might have gotten on, someone had stopped him brutally, and perhaps the time of fear wasn't over for the homeless.

"I guess this tells us something about the context." Cliff Waters held up the small plastic bag containing a white powder.

Ellie frowned. "That doesn't make sense. He didn't use or deal...no priors in that area."

"Perhaps no one had caught him yet, did you think about that? He got into it with someone. Remember what the park employee said. It's sad, but it seems this guy was always itching for a fight—this time, he picked the wrong people."

Ellie crouched down next to the victim. Marco Raynor's right hand was balled into a fist. She donned latex gloves, took a deep breath. And another.

"Go ahead," Dr. Adams told her.

Trying not to feel and hear what she was doing, Ellie carefully pried his fingers open, her stomach rolling slightly. A torn piece of paper came into view: part of a business card.

Her business card.

"Oh no." The words were out before she could hold them back.

"Don't make too much of it," Waters advised. "You gave it to him, right? It makes sense he still had it on him. Where else would he put it?"

"It's only part of it."

"Yeah, so? He tore it apart, obviously wasn't going to use it. Someone shot him. End of story."

"Maybe," Ellie said, aware of Dr. Adams rolling her eyes, and not at her. "Let's see if we have any prints. Dr. Adams, is it possible you move him to the top of the list?"

"I can move him further up," the medical examiner said. "If you don't have any plans for tonight?"

❦

Ellie pondered paying Bob Stanton another visit to ask him about making the rounds in Jayne's neighborhood. Instead, she decided to call, and, when he didn't answer, left him a message, asking him to contact her about the issue.

When she returned to the station, Ellie had several messages waiting for her, most of them having nothing to do with the case at hand. Kate asked to meet later. Ellie might not make it tonight, but she'd have to get back to her. There were some things left unspoken between them about planning a wedding together with Kate as the maid of honor, when Kate's own plans had been so tragically interrupted.

Madeline asked if she could help with anything. Ariel, who was working on her memoir with her aunt, wanted to know if Ellie and Jordan would like to read part of what she had written. Ellie was going to make time, and she knew that Jordan would, too. Jack and Pauline asked them to come over on the weekend.

Ellie had to smile. Her social calendar was fuller than it ever had been, with people who truly cared, and whom she cared about. She wished her parents could see this, see her truly happy.

She went to inform the lieutenant about their preliminary findings and after that, got herself a cup of coffee and began her own report. Waters was nowhere to be seen, but she was used to his patterns by now. She would ask when she needed to and otherwise leave him alone.

Maria Doss sat at her desk. Jordan and Derek were probably out on a case.

Ellie stared at the form in front of her, wondering what happened. She didn't believe that Marco was involved in any form of drug trade. Then again, she didn't know him that well. Could she rely on her gut instinct, or was she too hopeful about humanity in general, even after everything she had seen?

She was so lost in thought she hadn't heard Libby Marshall coming up behind her. Libby was working the front desk today.

"Hey, Ellie, do you have a moment? There's a Mr. Stanton here. He says he wants to talk to you."

"Sure." That was quick. Ellie wondered if she could play to the man's ego and make him think she was enlisting his help rather than working against him. She got up to follow Libby. Her colleague went back to her work while Ellie stepped through the door into the visitors' waiting area.

"Mr. Stanton, thank you for coming in right away. Please follow me?"

"Are you freaking kidding me?"

Libby was on her feet in an instant, looking alarmed.

"What do you mean?" Ellie had to admit she was confused. "Mr. Stanton, what's wrong?"

"You have the gall to..." He finally lowered his voice. "You treat honest citizens this way, you shouldn't be surprised if they turn against you one day."

"Let's talk about this. You don't want to be seen threatening a police officer."

"I'm not threatening anyone. I'm going to sue the hell out of this department. You keep overstepping your boundaries while all we do is try to protect the neighborhood from the lowlife lurking everywhere."

"I'm sorry, but that's not why I asked you here." Ellie had a hard time hiding her increasing irritation. "I thought that since you are keeping an eye on the neighborhood, you might be able to help. I'm sorry if I was mistaken."

"Help you how?" He tried to play it cool but sounded intrigued.

"How about we go somewhere we can sit down and talk?"

Still reluctant, but without further argument, he followed her to the other side of the door.

"You're going to be okay?" Libby asked.

"Yes, of course. It's just something we have to clear up."

They walked to her desk where she gestured for him to sit down. Detective Maria Doss cast them a curious look, then went back to whatever she was typing.

"I've been told you are trying to keep the drug trade out," Ellie began. "You must be aware of Mr. Ryan Lemont, then."

"Just what I read in the paper. He ran. Another one that got away from you, huh? If only you'd taken us seriously sooner."

Just like that, he was back to the insults. Ellie ignored them.

"One more thing. I'd like to see your firearm license again."

She didn't think Stanton could be stupid enough to shoot Marco Raynor with the same gun that already got him in trouble once—but she might get lucky.

Stanton bristled, but he handed over the document.

"Thank you, Mr. Stanton. That's just to double-check something."

"I know what you're getting at. That troublemaker in the park, he got himself shot. Can't say I'm going to shed a tear over him."

"You're not obliged. Let me make a copy of this, and that will be all."

"I sure as hell hope so."

She had no idea how to interpret his expression when she handed the document back to him.

"Thank you for your time."

"That's all right, Officer. I only aim to help."

"Detective," Ellie mumbled when he was out of earshot.

"That was odd," Maria commented. "Is he on your radar?"

Ellie cast a look at the copies she'd made.

"I didn't lie to him. I don't think this is the murder weapon, but it never hurts to check. Domestic abuser, charges were dropped. Maybe there's something."

"Yeah." Maria sighed. "Be careful what you wish for though. People like that can be pretty unpredictable."

"In some ways, they are sadly predictable. Damn. I think I need another coffee. It looks like I'll be here for a while."

Chapter Eleven

While Andrews Secure Living wasn't her case any longer, Jordan was happy to hear that the web was tightening around Andrews and his second in command. April had called her, excited to have new findings regarding the threatening emails to Mrs. Kenning. This was a close as they could get to finding justice for a desperate man and his widow.

Ellie was still stuck at work, and Derek had left before her, so Jordan made do with a frozen dinner and a glass of wine, surveying the never-ending to-do lists for the wedding.

What a wonderful coincidence that Ellie had been able to reconnect with her mother's friend—when it came to people and relationships, Ellie was definitely better at everything. Or perhaps she'd been lucky knowing better people early on. Leaning back on the couch, Jordan sighed to no one, exasperated with herself. What had possessed her to think that this time could be different, that Kathryn had magically turned into this responsible person who was ready to admit her mistakes and move beyond? Was that even an accurate assessment, or was she still looking at the situation through the eyes of the little girl that haunted her in her nightmares? Whose responsibility was it really to move beyond?

As usual, she found no satisfying answer. She wished that Ellie would come home soon—which was a hopeful and somewhat ironic development, after she had insisted on her space time after time. For a while, being by herself had been as necessary as breathing.

The doorbell rang, and for a moment, Jordan asked herself if the person on the other side of the door was someone she wanted to see. Slightly apprehensive, she opened the door, relieved when she saw Kate McCarthy.

"Hey. Come on in. Ellie isn't here yet, I'm afraid."

"Oh. She said she was waiting for the autopsy, but I didn't think it would take that long."

"She should be here soon. You can keep me company if you want and also keep me from drinking this wine all by myself."

Kate laughed. "That's an offer I can't refuse, then."

She left her coat and purse by the door and followed Jordan into the living area. Jordan went to get another glass. When she came back, she found Kate studying the items on the table dedicated to wedding arrangements.

"We're glad that you decided to come a little early," Jordan said. "It means a lot to Ellie." She was aware that there was a bit of an open ending to her statement. Kate had picked up on it too. She took the glass Jordan handed to her.

"Thank you. You are all very careful, and I appreciate that. It's not the easiest thing, but I've also realized there is no point in hiding away and becoming paranoid. What happened was tragic, and unfair and all, but I'm still alive. Pretending otherwise won't change anything. It won't bring Jensen back."

"That's true. We appreciate you being here—in every sense."

"Thanks." Kate sat down, flipping through one of the magazines. "I'm sure you're curious about something else."

"I am curious about many things," Jordan said, amused. "Not all of them are my business. You had some tough decisions to make."

"No kidding."

Jordan cast a look at her watch. "Look, I don't know how long it will take until Ellie gets here...but I can listen."

"Sure, why not? Ellie...She's amazing."

"No argument from me." They both laughed.

"I didn't think so. The thing is...She wants everyone to have their happy ending. It doesn't always work out that way. Sometimes, two people are together, you're on the same page, and it's fine. Not everything has to be like in the movies, a great love story."

"Are you on the same page?" Jordan asked.

Kate lifted her shoulders slightly. "I was hoping you could help me with that. You know Derek better than anyone. He's playing it cool. Is it going to break his heart that there won't be another wedding right after yours?"

"That's a tough one," Jordan admitted. Derek Henderson had been a bit of a player when she first met him, not that Jordan had any room to judge—at the time, or ever. The break-up with Kate had been tough on him, and she didn't think it was far-fetched to think he harbored some hopes for their relationship, now that it appeared to be on again. "He cares about you."

"Yeah. I know. I care about him too. I'm not sure I'm ready to say, this is it. Once you do that, things can be really scary."

"Tell me about it." That was something Jordan could relate to. Even though her relationship with Bethany had been largely dysfunctional, she never wanted anything bad to happen to her. They hadn't worked on the same cases that often, so they weren't always aware of the risks and dangers each of them faced.

With Ellie, it was different still. She couldn't imagine living without her, and that wasn't melodramatic.

"Make sure you know what you want. If it's to keep things casual, tell Derek. If you're walking away from something bigger, because you're scared...Don't. It's worth it. I promise."

"Wow. The scariest thing is that everything you just said makes sense. Things were going well, and I became terrified and ran."

"Well, you know better now—"

The doorbell rang again.

"This is a popular spot tonight," Jordan said. "Excuse me."

"Sure."

She walked to the door, wondering if this time it could be Ellie who had forgotten her keys, or had her hands full.

Instead, she opened the door to Kathryn, who, crying and shaking, hugged her closely before Jordan could step away.

"I am so sorry!"

The night had turned from interesting to surreal.

When Ellie finally got to gather her purse, coat and keys and go home, she had a lot to think about. Marco Raynor had cocaine on him, the same kind they'd seen over and over in that area. The biggest dealer: The elusive Ryan Lemont.

The amount Raynor had on him wasn't enough to suggest he wanted in on the business. How did he get his hands on it? He had no money.

Ellie cringed as another possibility came to mind.

Stanton's gun wasn't the same caliber as the one used in the shooting. That would have been too easy.

Waters had been present for most of the evening, though not much helpful. Ellie was beginning to figure out what his deal was: While she had worked most of her adult life to get here, to build a career, he couldn't wait to leave. He wasn't as blatant as Atwood, but he was the kind of person who was uncomfortable and irritated with change, buying into the fallacy that equality for all had to lead to disadvantages for some.

She wasn't going to try and change his mind. All Ellie had to do is wait a bit longer, and she might be partnered with Doss. That was something she looked forward to. For sure, she could learn a lot from Jordan, and already had...but it was easier to draw some lines with a woman she wasn't madly in love with.

Ellie smiled at the thought. She was looking forward to a quiet ending of the evening, just the two of them, maybe find creative ways to deal with the stress of the day.

*

"You were right all along. God, I have so much to make up for, I can't do it in a lifetime. I know that."

"Kathryn. Slow down."

Maybe there had been a hint of truth to what Kathryn had accused her of, and she was embarrassed by her upbringing. Jordan felt self-conscious right now, with Kate sitting not far away, and witnessing the scene. She wished she could make it through a conversation with her biological mother without having that younger self emerge, hurt and angry. Someone had to be the adult.

Kate got to her feet.

"It's late," she said. "I'll catch up with Ellie another time."

"That's fine. You can wait."

"I was hoping we could talk," Kathryn said tearfully. It wasn't until now that Jordan realized her hair and clothes were wet. She must have walked from the bus stop in the rain.

"Now? It's late. I'll have an early morning."

Kathryn's gaze fell on the table, the glasses half-filled with wine. Jordan almost expected her to make a comment about having time for drinks with friends despite the early morning. That was what Kathryn did—deflect.

"I am sorry about that, too, but I was hoping you could give me a few minutes. Then I'll leave you alone, I swear."

Jordan sighed. "All right. I'll make you a coffee."

"You don't have to…"

"Come on, before I change my mind."

Her cell phone vibrated on the table—a text message from Ellie to let her know she had left the department.

"This won't take long," she said to Kate. "Ellie's on her way."

She steered Kathryn towards the relative privacy of the kitchen area. "Okay, the guest bathroom's over there if you want to dry your hair a bit. I'll have the coffee ready in a bit."

"Thank you," Kathryn mumbled and disappeared into the bathroom.

Jordan busied herself with the coffee, not in the mood to explain anything to Kate. She took a mug out of the cabinet and placed it on the counter.

By the time Kathryn returned from the bathroom, she still had no idea what to expect—or what to say to her.

"Here. Sit down for a moment. Does Jim know you're here?"

In their own, unique, strange way, they seemed to care for each other a lot. More than they had ever cared for her.

"Yes, I left him a note. Jordan, I'm sorry for barging in, but there's something you need to know."

"Well, you're here now. What is it?"

"I know you probably don't believe me, but the drugs weren't mine."

"Come on."

Jordan, who had filled the cup for Kathryn, set it down with enough vehemence for some of the content to slosh over the rim. She tore a sheet from the roll of paper towels and wiped the counter.

"It's true. Jim has a little…rarely."

"Honestly? I don't care."

Kathryn poured a generous amount of milk into her coffee. Whether she liked it that way, or was stalling, Jordan couldn't tell.

"I stopped doing drugs years ago, and I haven't had a drink since before the tests at the hospital. I've had a few wake-up calls lately."

"And when CPS knocked on your door, that wasn't one of them?" Jordan asked icily.

Kathryn held her gaze. "Sadly, no, at the time it wasn't. I told you that already, but I thought it would be the best solution for everyone. Frankly—I don't know what could have happened. Each day just got worse. I had no more hope. There was no one I could ask for help, and if there had been, I wouldn't have known how to."

"You learned that, at least."

"We don't have much, but we were able to give shelter to some of those young women—Serena, when she was hiding from that Ryder guy. Meg. It's for them I would never have drugs lying around in the house..." She stopped, the impact of her words hitting them both.

"It's true, and it's horrible. I'm aware of it every day. I've learned to cook healthy meals and grow my own vegetables, and when the girls are around, I'll make sure there's nothing around to harm them. Back then..." She swallowed hard. "There was a time when I didn't care, about myself, about you. This is hard to admit, and I know it's harder for you. I don't need to be at the wedding. I just need you to know that I'm better now...and that I'm happy for you."

"Well, thanks."

Jordan wondered if she had asked herself the wrong questions all along. Kathryn had obviously embarked on a path that was good for her, living healthier, making amends.

Whether she succeeded or not, had little bearing on the challenges Jordan faced in her own life. Was she better? At taking care of herself, at being a partner? She winced at the memory of throwing the glass against the wall, not so long ago. Bethany, Valerie, and Ellie too, she had hurt them. While she hadn't cheated on Ellie and never would, her indecisiveness had come at a cost early on in their relationship.

If anything, she was grateful to Kathryn for showing her everything she hoped she'd never be—as a wife, and maybe, sometime in the future, as a mother. The old Kathryn, anyway. Jordan was still reeling at the notion of her birthmother having a vegetable garden and helping underprivileged girls in desperate situations. Kathryn, caring about someone, something other than chasing the next high.

"Anyway, that's all I wanted to say. Thanks for hearing me out."

"Wait. I can drive you."

"I can still catch the bus—"

"Just let me do it, okay?"

Ellie came home to find Kate almost asleep on the couch, an empty glass of wine in front of her. A cup with a rest of coffee sat on the kitchen counter.

"Hi. It's good to see you, but it's not quite what I expected. Jordan isn't here?"

"Her mother came to visit, and she drove her home," Kate explained.

"Pauline? Is something wrong?"

"Oh no, it was Mrs. Larson."

"What did she want?" Ellie asked without thinking. Kate's perplexed expression spoke volumes.

"I'm not sure I know, but I think she came to apologize for something. You have to ask Jordan about the rest."

"I will. Sorry." Ellie hoped that this was a good development. At this point, she found it hard to tell if it was better for Jordan to stay in touch with Kathryn—or not.

"Speaking of mothers," Kate continued, "I heard you found a friend of yours? How did that go?"

"Pretty well. She and her family are really nice, considering that I've ignored them for the past few years." Ellie sat next to her friend.

"I'm sure they understood your reasons."

"I'm lucky they did. But there was something you wanted to talk about?"

"Don't worry, Jordan and I discussed this already. Just know that I'm really, truly excited to help you out any way I can, and I swear I'm not going to start sobbing anywhere in the process."

"Wow, I missed a lot."

Kate smiled gently. "Not so much, but I think I should go home now. I looked at some of those magazines. Do you know what you'll be wearing? The date is getting closer, and there might be alterations necessary..."

Truth be told, Ellie hadn't been able to make a lot of time for those considerations. "We got the invitations out, and the venue booked. I thought that was some success."

Kate laughed. "You've got to wear something. What do you think, we get Pauline and Libby and go this weekend? I'd enlist Derek as well, but he'd just say to go with the first one we try, so that's not an option."

"I'm so glad you're here." Ellie hugged her the moment the key turned in the front door's lock, and Jordan walked in, looking tired.

"Anyone else need a ride?"

"It's late," Ellie said. "Kate, would you like to crash here? We could talk more over breakfast."

"If it's not too much trouble?"

"Not at all. I'll make pancakes."

***

"How tired are you?" Ellie asked as she ran a fingertip down Jordan's back, satisfied when her action caused a pleasant shiver.

"Hm, I'm not sure if that's the right question," Jordan murmured. "We have a guest."

"Who's two rooms away, which is farther than it was in the apartment. If I remember correctly, that didn't stop us."

Jordan turned to her, smiling. "I'm good. You are the less...quiet one."

"Now you're bragging," Ellie challenged, knowing Jordan wouldn't be able to resist. True to experience, she found herself pinned down a moment later, sighing happily.

"God, I've been dreaming about this all day. Is it okay if we talk about work, Kathryn, and everything else tomorrow?"

"Fine with me," Jordan whispered against her neck, her hand wandering underneath the hem of her nightgown, brushing the inside of her thigh. Ellie bit her lip and then thought twice about it. Two rooms were enough of a distance. She wasn't that loud, regardless of Jordan's teasing. The caresses continued, and Jordan gently removed the nightgown, tossing it aside as she brushed her lips against the uncovered skin.

"Thank you."

For a moment, Ellie wasn't sure what to make of the quiet words.

"I needed this, too."

***

That night, Jordan dreamed about the Prophets of Better Days compound, and the day they'd found Ariel, one of the many girls under constant threat of getting "married" to one of the older men. Jordan's dreamscape changed to a later moment when Ariel had run away shortly after her rescue. She'd been overwhelmed by the outside world that was safer but also came with many responsibilities and decisions she never had to make before. Ellie and Jordan had found her not far from her home.

Jordan held dream-Ariel close, telling her that everything would be all right. She was both in awe and mildly disturbed when Ariel morphed into another, even younger girl. The image vanished into nothing, and she woke with a start.

Over breakfast, she reflected on the dream listening to Kate and Ellie discuss colors for bridesmaid dresses. She didn't need a shrink to interpret it though both Bethany and Dr. Burns, whom she'd seen for a while after her run-in with a serial killer, would likely have a field day with this. The bottom line—things were good. She didn't have to take care of Kathryn—then, or now. As a child, she had done everything she could to keep herself safe.

No more nightmares, and she had a beautiful and loving woman by her side who was about to become her wife...life couldn't get much better, but it did.

The pancakes Ellie had promised were amazing too.

Chapter Twelve

Finally, a break presented itself in the form of one of Ryan Lemont's dealers, a man called Ethan James. He had worked for Lemont on a number of occasions, and one of them, as it turned out, had been two weeks ago. When Casey and Potts picked him up, he was more than eager to flip on Lemont and provide the authorities with an address.

Within minutes, Ellie and Waters were on their way to the motel where Lemont was hiding out. The place was nondescript, not one of the cheapest ones either.

The receptionist's eyes widened in shock when they presented their badges, but she gave them the key without protest. They didn't have to warn her twice to stay inside.

Ellie and Waters made their way up a flight of stairs. On the balcony that connected the upstairs rooms, they stayed close to the wall as they approached the door of Lemont's room. Ellie's heart was beating hard in her chest. The drug dealer was a violent man, and he was without a doubt armed. There was no saying what he would do if he felt cornered.

Her worst fears weren't confirmed though: The door opened, and a surly looking Ashley stepped outside.

"What is it with you cops? I told you I don't know where—"

He pushed Ashley aside and ran across the balcony to the stairs on the other side, trying to make it to his car.

Ellie immediately gave chase, hearing Waters notify Casey and Potts, and call for backup. Lemont managed to get into his car, but their backup arrived with blazing sirens, stopping their vehicles in a way he couldn't get out.

"Mr. Lemont? Get out of the car," she shouted, advancing on his car. "Hands in the air!"

He had nowhere to go. After a few tense moments, practically vibrating with anger, he stepped out of the car, and Ellie put the cuffs on him.

"Thanks," she said to her uniformed colleagues who had blocked the exit. "If you could give this gentleman a ride downtown?"

Ashley came running down the stairs as well.

"What are you doing?"

"Hiding your ex-boyfriend who jumped bail gives us enough reason to invite you along," Waters told her.

"I didn't do anything!"

"Sure, we'll talk about that in a moment. Let's see what we find in that motel room."

Another squad car arrived as Waters was speaking, Libby and Wes emerging.

"You missed all the action," Casey told them, "but you can take her."

"That's Ryan Lemont in there?" Libby asked. "Damn, Ellie, you're having the best month ever."

"You have to give Sam and Casey some credit." Though she hadn't seen her often lately, Ellie had at least found out that Potts's name was Sam. "They found him."

"All right, if you're done with your little tea party, can we get back to work?" Waters grumbled.

Casey shook her head and turned around. Officer Potts joined her in the car, and they drove off.

"He made me come here," Ashley insisted. "He had a gun."

"My colleagues are going to clear up all of this with you. Please come with us now," Libby told her.

Ellie and Waters went back up the stairs and into the motel room. He looked irritated. Ellie couldn't fathom why—they had arrested Lemont without either of them having to fire a shot. That was a success in her book.

"Is everything all right?" she finally asked.

"Yeah. Just pay attention."

That was what she did, every day, all day. Perhaps now was not the time to prod. They quickly searched the room, finding two bags filled with envelopes like the one Marco Raynor had carried with him.

"There you go," Waters muttered.

"What do you mean? We don't know that Marco Raynor bought from Lemont. He had no money to speak of, why would Lemont give him drugs for free?"

"Maybe he was running drugs for him? Or girls?"

Ellie shook her head even as she considered his theory. None of the homeless persons she talked to, including Marco himself, had given her that impression, but then again, there were still many pieces missing.

"Let's see what Lemont tells us."

Waters didn't protest which she interpreted as approval.

⚬

"Never saw him."

Lemont had barely looked at the picture Ellie showed him once they were settled in the interrogation room.

"Try again," she urged. "Perhaps he approached you for drugs or—" Stole from you? She suppressed a sigh. It didn't make sense.

"Bullshit," Waters scoffed. "Cocaine isn't easy to come by in this neighborhood, but if someone has it, chances are it was yours. You're the go-to guy now, isn't that true?"

Lemont took another look and shrugged. "Whatever you say. If I was still in the business, which you have no proof of, I surely wouldn't do business with a guy like him. You might remember that my clientele was a little more...high profile."

Ellie had read in the file that when he was first arrested, a politician and a TV personality had been questioned. He was clearly bragging, but he did have a point.

"Until the neighborhood watch drove you out of town."

"What are you talking about? I was taking a break..."

"Jumping bail..."

He shook his head, amused. "You all misunderstood. I wasn't that hard to find, was I? I wanted to talk to Ashley in private...no one drives me out of town."

Ellie hadn't forgotten what Jayne had told her. Had Stanton and his gang made some deal with him?

Could it be possible that she was wrong—if only because she wanted Stanton to be guilty of something? She had to do better than that. Especially since the initial warrant on Lemont had been out on something completely unrelated to the neighborhood watch.

Perhaps she had to let this one go.

"Okay," she said.

He shot her an incredulous look.

"That's what you brought me here for? Lady, any lawyer fresh out of law school would make a nice case against you."

"I don't think so. There's still the matter of you running away...and your DNA at the scene of a murder."

He shook his head with a grim smile. "Don't think I haven't heard that bluff before. Hey. Is she new or something?" he addressed Waters.

"I think you didn't hear the question she asked you, so let's try this again. We can put you at the scene of a murder. Ashley might be a little more cooperative too, when she knows you'll be going away for a long time. So, what is it going to be?" In the resulting silence, Waters added, "I'll give you some time to think about it. You still don't want to talk, maybe your friend Bobby Stanton will. After all, he might get away with a slap on the wrist. You won't. Come on, Harding."

He motioned for her to follow him, and Ellie did. Lemont's grin didn't go unnoticed with her.

"Not my friend!" he called after them. "I still have no idea what you're talking about."

"Do you believe Stanton could be involved?" she asked once they were outside of the room.

"We know that he has some sway in the neighborhood. I'm pretty sure they have crossed paths."

Ellie was fairly surprised at the conciliatory tone, but she'd take it. This was a high-profile case. Any time Waters didn't tell her to shut up and follow his lead she imagined she was on a good path.

Speaking of which...she was glad Jordan had figured out some things of a more private nature as well, as another important date would be coming up the next day. Ellie readily admitted that she was one of those women who'd been dreaming about it from the time she was a little girl.

Jordan didn't have much time to obsess about the dress shopping, her mind on many other things, first and foremost on how she'd handled the Kathryn situation. Saturday morning seemed to arrive all of a sudden, and Ellie was already off with Kate while

Jordan had breakfast with Pauline. Libby would join them later to play her part in the elaborate plan.

"What a beautiful day," Pauline said as she hugged her at the door. "Come on in. I can tell you from experience that this will take a while, so we need some sustenance first."

Jordan had to chuckle at the sight of the breakfast table.

"I'm scared. If I eat all of that, I don't think I'll fit into any of those dresses."

"You'll be fine. Let's sit. There's plenty of time until your appointment."

That much was true—Ellie had been struck with a sudden bolt of superstition, and she didn't want them to see each other's dresses before the wedding day. Jordan played along, even though she thought that as long as Ellie wasn't going to run, they'd be fine.

"So, tell me everything," Pauline urged after she'd poured coffee for both of them. "What are we looking for? Long, short, sleeves, no sleeves—pantsuit? I have to warn you, I might cry. And again during the ceremony, and a few more times along the way."

"A dress is okay. I have to admit I haven't given it much thought to it otherwise."

"Oh honey, this is really going to take all day." Pauline laughed, her eyes already welling up. "I don't mind. I am so happy for you."

"I am happy for me, too. I don't think any of us saw that coming."

"To be honest, I wasn't sure if that's what you wanted. You were with Bethany a long time, and neither of you ever seemed to mention the subject. Then again, things are very different now."

"They are."

Pauline never pushed, but her observation skills had always allowed her to gauge Jordan's state of mind. Even if there were many things Jordan had never told her. She knew she could have, but she had decided early that with her and Jack, the people who had first given her an idea of stability, she had to keep some space that was untainted.

Spare them, spare herself. Pauline knew she'd had nightmares the first few years, which had as much to do with missing Jim and Kathryn as fearing someone could send her back. She never told her or Jack that often, she lay awake, bewildered by the quiet around her that was so different from everything she knew. In the early days, it was that quiet that had robbed her of sleep.

As much as she struggled with Kathryn in her life, Jordan was also aware that she'd found some missing pieces in the relationship with her biological parents, however complicated. But Kathryn wasn't here to help her pick a wedding dress. She would share that experience with the woman who had always been there for her, from the day they met.

"I'm really happy we are doing this together," she said, her throat going tight.

Pauline smiled gently. "Me too."

They finished their breakfast together and left for the store after Jordan received a text message from Libby that said she was on her way, and then there was no more reprieve. She had to admit the many different shades of white, blush—she'd learned that from one of the bridal magazines—and a few other colors were intimidating. At least the employee that greeted them cheerily seemed to know what she was doing, making suggestions, and stepping into the dressing room with Jordan, because there was no way a person could get into any of those gowns by herself. It was okay, she reflected, going better than expected. So far, she hadn't been overly impressed. Pauline wasn't crying yet, and Libby looked as if she was facing a serious, complicated task.

She wondered how Ellie's appointment was going. Then again Ellie was extremely focused with matters like this, and picking a pretty dress and shoes was nothing out of the ordinary for her.

The employee, Caitlyn, brought another dress and patiently helped Jordan get out of the one she was wearing, and into the new one. "You said no frills. This one just came in this morning. Hm. I think you could wear your hair down with it. Did you discuss hairstyles with your fiancée?"

"Um...I can't say we have." Did that list never end? Obediently, she pulled the tie out of her hair, thinking that she was grateful for Pauline's foresight. This was taking forever. Perhaps they could meet the other half of their party for a late lunch somewhere. Jordan caught a glimpse of herself in the mirror, her jaw dropping. Caitlyn looked satisfied with herself. "Let's go show your mom and friend, okay?"

Strange, how the fact apparently hadn't hit home until the moment—this was happening, a once-in-a-lifetime event, something permanent. She saw Pauline wiping her eyes, and Libby's face lighting up.

"Jackpot," she said.

"I think we found the one." Caitlyn beamed at her. "What do you say?"

"I like it. I really do. Could you excuse me for a moment?" With that, she headed back to the dressing room, Caitlyn on her heels.

"Please," Jordan said. She barely avoided shutting the door in the young woman's face, feeling bad, but she could always apologize later. Other things couldn't wait. She took her cell phone out of the pocket of her coat and swiped through her address book. Waiting for the recipient of the call to pick up, she regarded herself once more in the mirror, spooked beyond reason.

They were right.

Jackpot.

"Hey," Derek said. "I thought you were busy this morning?"

"Where are you?"

"Currently reading the paper on my balcony. Is everything okay?"

"I need you to come and get me. Say it's about work, something that can't wait."

"Now I'm worried. That doesn't sound okay."

Jordan wasn't sure what to answer to that. "Can I count on you?"

"Of course. Text me the address, and don't give too many details if you want us to keep our stories straight."

"Thank you. I really appreciate it."

"I know you do. See you there."

True to his word, Derek arrived not much later with a plausible cover story that didn't make Jordan look too bad. She excused herself and promised everyone to give the dress some more thought.

When they sat in Derek's car, she breathed a sigh of relief.

"So, what happened? Did they poke you with the pins?"

With some distance from the shop and high expectations, she could relax a bit.

"Give me a minute? I need to check what Ellie's at, so she doesn't worry." She wrote a quick text message to let Ellie know she'd meet her later at Jack and Pauline's.

"Is there something to worry about?"

Jordan wasn't sure how to answer that, so she didn't.

"Did you have lunch yet? I'm starving. I'll buy," she added when Derek gave her a quizzical look.

"Not necessary," he said. "Are you going to tell me?"

When I figure it out, she thought. Derek knew her better than most people, but then it was still hard to explain why her reflection had freaked her out this much. The perfect dress for the perfect day. It seemed like an illusion, utterly unattainable.

"What if I suck at this?" she blurted out.

"What, being mysterious? You're pretty good at it. I haven't got a clue."

"Funny. I mean, marriage. Happy ever after."

Derek pulled into the narrow parking spot in front of the restaurant.

"Okay, what's that supposed to mean? Last time I checked you were pretty happy. You guys bought a house, you wanted to adopt a child...now, what? Wait, don't tell me..."

"No. No! Of course not. I have no doubts about Ellie. I love her."

"It's probably just nerves," he offered. "I imagine there's quite a bit to do in the weeks to come."

"That's not it. What I mean is...look where I come from. My mother cheated. I did. I've done a few things I'm not proud of, and...Ellie makes all the smart decisions. She could do so much better."

"Are you even listening to yourself?"

At this moment, Jordan wasn't even sure what point she was trying to make, but it was something that still rang true. No matter how hard she had tried to push the feeling aside.

"Well, Bethany said so. Speaking about herself, not Ellie, that is."

"Yeah, that's another reason why I don't like her."

"She had a point." If that were true for Bethany, maybe it was true for Kathryn as well. In the present, Kathryn had found young women for whom she wanted to be a parental figure.

Maybe she, too, thought she could do better, that Jordan wasn't good enough for her.

"No, she didn't. She could have ended it, but she worked your guilt for all it was worth. As for your birthmother, she managed to stay married after all, and so did your parents. If you really want to go there, then you have nothing to worry about."

Jordan admitted to herself that she hadn't considered this angle. It was strange to think of Kathryn as someone to look to for anything, but it was true—she had managed to maintain her marriage all through her turbulent life. Regardless of all the mistakes she'd made, and there were plenty, she had recently helped young women in a desperate situation. So, was it okay to pick and choose?

"I can't believe I did this," she said ruefully. "I mean...This is my responsibility, right? It's up to me not to screw it up, not Kathryn, or Bethany."

"Exactly. Now what is this case we're supposed to be working? We better keep our stories straight for the dinner party later."

It took Jordan a moment to understand why they'd be going to the same dinner party at Pauline's, then she made the connection.

"So, you and Kate are definitely on again," she stated.

"We're taking it slow. That's all I can tell you."

"That's probably a good idea," Jordan said, remembering her conversation with Kate. "Okay. Thank you for this. I owe you one conversation in case of a freak-out."

He shook his head, amused. "We're good."

Chapter Thirteen

E llie was in love with everything about this day, even through traces of melancholy kept creeping in as she imagined how much her parents would have liked to share it with her. They wouldn't be able to see her make a commitment to the woman she loved, officially, legally. She was grateful that Madeline was here.

When Kate received a text message from Derek about working a case with Jordan, out of the blue, she wasn't sure what to make of it, but Ellie did have an idea.

Not that she could do anything about it now.

She distracted herself with a mental to-do list for the beginning of the following week. Waters had decided that he didn't consider Stanton a person of interest in the murders of Marco Raynor and the waitress, Rena Kelly, after all. Fortunately, Ellie had friends in the department, and she'd continue to ask around unobtrusively. True, she didn't like Stanton for his attitude and his history of domestic violence. That alone, she knew, would be hard to sell as a reason to continue digging. Associating with a major league drug dealer would work, and if that saved another woman who might otherwise get involved with this man, even better.

She cast another look at her mirror image.

Ellie knew that at whatever point it was they had arrived, she and Jordan had earned it, every bit of it. She suspected that Jordan had seen something slightly different in the mirror.

By the time they found each other at Pauline's, Ellie had to admit that the day's activities, while worth-while, had been exhausting. She had tried many different dresses until finding the one and was now hungry and grateful for a place to sit, and the glass of wine Jordan brought her.

"So, what was the emergency?" she asked when Jordan sat down next to her. Ellie could tell by Jordan's slightly guilty expression that she was on the right track.

"It's kind of hard to explain."

Perhaps it was, for Jordan, in the light of day, from an adult perspective. It was also fairly easy.

"Did you find a dress?"

"I did."

"That's good news, right?" Ellie wasn't going to drag out a conversation that was clearly uncomfortable for Jordan. She had a suspicion as to why, but she needed a little more information. "There was no case, was there?"

Jordan leaned back against the headrest and sighed. "I suppose Derek didn't have to tell you. I'm really sorry. You know it doesn't mean I don't want this."

"I know. What does it mean?"

"Nothing. Can't we just forget about it?"

"Just bear with me for a moment, okay? I might be wrong, but I think you saw something perfect, and it startled you, because you didn't think it could be for you, ever."

"That sounds disturbingly right." Jordan shook her head. "It doesn't make sense. Perhaps I should make another appointment with the shrink."

"It's all good. We'll figure it out together, and meanwhile, just believe me that you deserve everything perfect. We do. I love you."

Ellie leaned in for a quick kiss, aware that she was choking herself up. How would she ever make it through the wedding vows?

It came to no surprise when, the next morning, Ellie found out that she was on her own for the workday. She didn't mind either. Her partner's absence bode well for her plans, but there was something she needed to do first. After a quick run to the coffee shop across the street, she went straight to Detective Doss's desk.

"Do you have a moment?"

Maria Doss looked up from the file she was reading, and, seeing Ellie holding a tray with two tall coffees and muffins, she obviously decided the answer was yes.

"Sit, please. We have a chance to make all of this disappear before the lieutenant comes back from his meeting. Where's your partner?"

"Taking a half day today," Ellie told her.

Doss didn't look surprised. "What do you need?"

"I could use some advice, but since Cliff isn't here, I was wondering if you could tell me something...If he says to let go of something, is it usually legit?"

"Straight to the point. Look, I can't give you a general answer here, but I guess you already found out that he does his own thing. He's not especially keen on hearing other people's opinions, especially when those people are female. Does that help?"

"Kind of," Ellie admitted. "I have noticed that before, and it's definitely still true."

"When we first started working together, he asked me if my brother was in a gang. My brother is an accountant and unlike me, has never seen a gun or a gang member up close, but that's what Waters does. He goes just far enough to annoy you, not enough to get fired. I almost felt sorry for you when the lieutenant assigned you to him, but frankly, not sorry enough. I enjoy work quite a bit more now. At least it won't be too long for you with his retirement coming up." She held up her cup. "And this is why I shouldn't talk to anyone before the first coffee. Sorry about that."

"It's okay." If anything, Ellie was getting nothing but confirmation that she'd be doing the right thing. "Look, there's this guy who seems to be on the periphery of a case, but I have nothing solid yet. I wonder how far I can go on a hunch."

"That depends on how relevant you think they are. Are you sure they're going to lead to something? Do more of the footwork and then bring it to Esposito. If you bring her something good enough, she'll give you the warrants."

"Hm."

"Do absolutely nothing without a warrant." Maria had misinterpreted her reaction.

"I know, I know. I think I have an idea."

"Perhaps Cliff's half day is a good opportunity to follow up on that, if you think it's a good use of taxpayer money."

"Oh, I'm sure it is. Thank you, Maria."

"No problem. Thanks for the snack."

"I hope you understand I couldn't discuss this with Jordan." Ellie wasn't sure she'd meant to reveal this, but Maria nodded.

"It's okay. Dating within the same department can be tricky, and you're new, but don't worry. I think you're doing just fine."

"Thanks." Ellie got to her feet and picked up her own coffee. "You've helped a lot."

Back at her own desk, she went once more over the statements of Ryan Lemont, Jayne, and Ashley. Was there a connection between Marco Raynor and Lemont after all? Jayne seemed to have been grateful for the watch "cleaning up the neighborhood," cracking down on drug dealers. Her apartment and Ashley's were within less a mile from one another, both of them within the area that might have been on the radar of Bob Stanton and his friends. In one direction, Patton Lake Park, tourist accommodations and expensive condos, in the other, a more forgotten neighborhood with a high amount of crime threatening to spill over into the more picturesque surroundings close by. She needed a more detailed picture to figure out who had killed Raynor, and if his death was at all related to the neighborhood watch. At the same time, Ellie didn't want to miss anything if there was any kind of wrongdoing on the group's part.

She took some notes to take with her and went to find Casey and Sam Potts.

"Hey there. I need a bit of help finding potential witnesses," she began, a bit awkward with her friend and the new rookie. In her mind, Ellie was amused at herself. When she had still been in uniform, the detectives never seemed to worry about asking for additional personnel. And this was important, not just a hunch of hers. Marco Raynor was a victim who deserved justice like any other.

Fortunately, the two officers had no intention of arguing with her, and so she showed them Ashley's and Jayne's apartments on the map, and the area in which she wanted to explore more of the neighborhood watch's reach, and the neighbors' opinion on it.

"I want to know if they've seen Stanton and the others around, and if the presence is a helpful or a threatening one. Bring everything to me."

"Sure, no problem," Casey answered for the two of them. Sam looked excited. "We'll meet you there?"

"Yes. I'm going to start with Ashley."

"You again. What do you want? I already told you everything, and so did Jayne. I just want to put all of this behind me, is that too much to ask?"

Ellie waited until Ashley had finished. She could certainly understand about wanting to leave traumatic experiences in the past—but it was also her experience that unless you had illuminated every corner of the story, it could always come back to haunt you.

"I understand. Please hear me out," she added when Ashley scoffed. "I know you want to get your life back on track, and that will work best if Ryan can't interfere with it anymore. He's not giving up much, but we know he has contacts in the area. Jayne told us about the neighborhood watch." If some of them were working with Lemont, these types could be just as dangerous to Ashley or women like her. Ellie didn't say that out loud. She waited until her words had sunk in.

"If you're telling me to move, forget about it. I can't afford it. As long as you keep Ryan behind bars, I'll be okay. If he gets out...Well, you know what happened to that waitress. I didn't tell on him, but don't think that will make a difference."

"We hope to make a difference, for everyone in this community."

Ashley laughed bitterly. "Because of the tourists nearby?"

"Because it's our job to serve and protect everyone, and we hope that you can trust us again," Ellie insisted. She couldn't blame the woman for her defeatist attitude. Apparently, the police hadn't been much of a help to anyone around here in recent years. "That neighborhood watch Jayne mentioned, are you aware of them?"#1

"Vaguely." Ashley shrugged. "I know there was talk about how they might be involved with the homeless folks' deaths. That's a shame, anyway. They didn't hurt anyone."

"I agree. I understand there have been altercations, though the members of the watch weren't involved in those murders. Is there anything else you can tell me about them? Did you ever see Ryan with one of them, or did he talk to you about them?"

"I value being alive, so I never asked much about his business," Ashley said. "He was laughing at them. He said that if they wanted to clean up the neighborhood, they'd have to start with themselves. I didn't press him on details."

"Did you discuss the situation with any neighbors, friends...Jayne?"

Another shrug. "Look, it's a rough neighborhood. You try to avoid the guys with the guns, regardless of what their intention might be. It's safer. I know Jayne doesn't see it that way, but in my opinion it's nothing but a pissing contest. They haven't helped anyone."

"Thank you, Ashley. If you can think of anything else, please call me."

"Sure."

Ellie could tell from her tone that a call wasn't likely. A tad disappointed, she left the apartment, turning around on the front stairs to see movement behind the window. From the start, she'd been sure that Ashley hadn't told her the whole story.

She was on her way to meet with Sam and Casey when she got the text message.

Don't ever tell her I gave you her name, but you should talk to Addy. Folks tried to clean out her block. Ellie fed the address into her GPS and texted Casey to meet in an hour.

For all the smoke and mirrors, Addy Henson put two and two together quickly. She stayed behind the chain, door locked, casting a suspicious look at Ellie's badge.

"I'm not sure what Ashley is thinking, but I have no desire or reason to talk to the police," she said, giving it back.

"Could I come in?"

"If you have a warrant, sure."

Ellie straightened her shoulders. "You've done nothing wrong, but it would really help me if you could answer some questions. It might help Ashley too."

"Seems like Ashley's doing whatever she can to help herself these days." Addy shrugged and removed the chain. "Come on in," she said, opening the door wide. "Better than me being seen talking to you."

Ellie followed her into the modest apartment, aware that she had no time to waste.

"Do you know a Bob Stanton?" she asked. Addy spun around, an expression of disbelief and shock on her face. So she did.

"Why? I thought this was about Ashley and the drug dealer she was dating."

"It is. So you know Mr. Stanton."

"You could say that. Ashley isn't the only one who made bad choices, but I figured it out pretty quickly. There's a reason why his ex didn't get her day in court."

"You were in a relationship? He abused you too?" Ellie felt queasy summing up the likely course of events.

Addy slumped onto the worn green couch.

"He's the kind of guy who gets away with it. He always has his buddies with him, and they're all carrying. Why be foolish?"

The sensation of nausea gave way to anger, as Ellie found more and more confirmation for her theory. How many women lived in fear in this area? She had checked Bob Stanton's license before, and she assumed the other members of the watch all had legit gun permits. That angle, unfortunately, would get her nowhere.

As much as she wanted to take action, right away, it would take something solid to make the higher-ups understand about this epidemic of domestic violence. Worse, they might be wary of opening that can of worms after the authorities had just shut down a sect that had been operating under the radar for decades.

"I want to make sure that this time, he doesn't get away with it," she said. "But I need you to help me. I assume that Bob's friends clashed with the drug dealers at times. Do you know if they did drugs themselves?"

"They mostly drank and went out looking for trouble. But Ashley's boyfriend came over once, and they talked for a long time."

"Friendly?"

"Business kind of friendly. I don't think Bob was interested in buying some pot for a party. He always had big ideas, about making money quick."

For their insistence not wanting to talk to the police, it seemed to be a relief to both Ashley and Addy that someone was listening to them—perhaps for the first time.

"Do you have any proof, pictures, a recording, anything of the two of them together?" Ellie's heart beat faster. If she could link Stanton to Lemont, it would be to the detriment of both of them. They could clean up the neighborhood and make it safer for its residents—just not according to the business model the two men might have had in mind.

"Are you crazy? Either one of them would have killed me if I had tried that. You know about the waitress, and no one has any idea what happened to that ex-wife."

"All right, something else. Is Bob the leader in that neighborhood watch? Did you meet any other members, or know who has the authority?"

"Only when they needed someone to cook for them. They pretty much look the same, brooding guys who think everyone is taking something away from them—you know, the sluts and the gays and the immigrants. Funny how they always find someone to blame for their shit other than themselves."

Ellie could only agree, but she was excited to finally get somewhere. "You have names?"

"Sure. And...I don't know if that's important, but there was this nineteen-year-old, always leering at me. He was there for the meeting with Ryan as well, and he idolized Bob. His name's...Jarrod, I think, Jarrod Tanner."

It took Ellie a few seconds to remember where she'd heard that name before. He'd been on the list of students who had volunteered for the program to work with the homeless in the park—according to the list, he had only attended once. Since Norton and Heller had confessed to murder and arson respectively, there had been no need to go back to that list. Now, she wondered if she might have overlooked something.

"This is all very good. Thanks so much for making time for me, Addy."

"Well...it doesn't happen every time that the police come around to actually listen what we have to say. I guess it goes both ways."

"I'll do my best to make sure you won't have to worry about them any longer, and Ashley as well," Ellie promised.

Back in her car, she gathered her map and notes once more, adding points according to the interviews. A picture was emerging, but she still needed physical proof to put Lemont and Stanton in the same room. She needed to find out more about Jarrod Tanner and pay him a visit, but she'd have to confer with Casey and Sam first and then head back to the station to see what Waters was up to.

If it was true that Lemont and Stanton had worked together, it made sense for them to involve someone younger, a contact in a school or college. It was a truly clever and devious plan—the pretense to drive out crime while cutting deals with one particular player. Both men would benefit from it. Stanton and his neighborhood watch could present some successes, and Lemont could get rid of a big part of the competition.

Until they'd start to eat their own. Getting too close to people like that could come back to seriously bite you, not that Ellie felt sorry for a group of self-pitying violent misogynists.

Chapter Fourteen

"**Y**ou have any idea where your girlfriend is?" Waters grumbled as Jordan passed by his desk. "Not taking the job so seriously after she couldn't wait to have it. I see."

She could see the flash of annoyance on Maria Doss's face.

"She's out working," Maria said. "You know, detective work."

Jordan secretly enjoyed the exchange, deciding she didn't need to add anything to it.

Waters wasn't placated. "I didn't tell her to go out. There are five open cases, and she's on a wild goose chase. I don't need that."

"Well, perhaps Jordan can help you. She doesn't look busy."

Not so amused now, Jordan made a slightly obscene gesture in Maria's direction, behind Waters' back.

She couldn't deny the truth of Maria's statement though.

"Sure, what do you need?"

"For Harding to show up, now. You'd help me a lot if you could get her here."

"All right, relax. I'll call her."

If Ellie was out investigating by herself, Jordan was certain she had a good reason. She hoped that it wouldn't get her into trouble with Lieutenant Carroll. She saw Maria's thoughtful gaze, wondering if she knew more.

Fortunately, the moment she clicked on Ellie's number, Ellie walked in, Casey and Officer Potts in tow.

"Harding," Waters barked. "It's already late, now get your ass over here."

His words caused a collective cringe from the women in the room, a reaction that he ignored. Jordan had a hard time not to interfere, even though she knew for certain Ellie could handle herself.

"Hey, Cliff, I'm sorry," she said with a shrug. "I need to finish up with these officers first. I think we have a few new leads."

Jordan hadn't missed Maria smiling to herself.

"What part of get your ass over here didn't you understand?"

No one was smiling at this point, and the lieutenant had come out of his office as well.

"Waters, Harding, a word?" His tone made it clear that this was not a suggestion. At least it would be mostly Waters who would have to explain himself, Jordan assumed.

"Retirement can't come soon enough," Maria commented.

❦

Cliff Waters left the lieutenant's office fuming, stopping short at slamming the door. Ellie hastily got to her feet. She didn't care that he was mad at her, but she didn't want his foul mood to slow down the progress she'd made.

"Harding, wait a minute."

She sat back down, feeling herself tense up with worry. What could this be about? So far, Lieutenant Carroll seemed on board with her line of investigation, though he had warned her he needed to see results soon if the inquiries extended into the neighborhood watch and its connections to Lemont.

Ellie understood that, and she was sure she could provide these connections if Waters let her do her work.

"Yes, sir?"

"Are you planning on filing a complaint?"

The question caught her off guard.

"What...no, I don't think so. Detective Waters disagrees on how to handle this case. I understand I'm still new to this, but—"

"I wasn't talking about the case. There's a fine line between a joke gone too far, and harassment, and I would hate for one of my detectives to be on the wrong side of that."

"I appreciate your concern, but I'm fine, really."

Lieutenant Carroll didn't prod. "I'm glad to hear that," he said. "Good job."

"Thank you."

"And make sure those leads are being followed. We can't let these people down once more, or they'll never trust us again."

"I'll do that."

Ellie left the office lost in thought, feeling strangely awkward as she returned to her colleagues. It hadn't even crossed her mind that she could bring Waters' behavior, should it escalate from here, to a superior. Truth be told, she had found it annoying and stifling with regard to the job. Since Maria Doss had toughed it out for so long, Ellie, being the newbie, didn't want to rock the boat, especially when it came to a fellow cop.

All of a sudden, she understood a whole lot more about why it was so hard for Ashley, Addy, and many other women to trust the authorities...Perhaps they had before, and it changed nothing about their situation.

This wasn't true for Ellie though. She had people in her life that had her back—and she'd do whatever she could to make sure those women could live without fear as well.

"I want to talk to Lemont again, see if I can shake him a little, make him think the deal with the neighborhood watch is off. And I want to pay this Jarrod guy a visit. It's probably not a coincidence that he was involved in the university program, if only briefly. He might want to turn on either one of them."

"It's not going to be so easy if Stanton is his idol," Jordan reminded her. In a quieter corner of the *Night Shift*, they were hashing out the day. To Waters' chagrin, the lieutenant had approved more personnel on the Raynor/Stanton/Lemont case.

"Yeah, but maybe there's a chance he could establish himself if Stanton were gone. There is a good chance that we can play them all against one another, and I have this feeling that Jarrod is the weaker link."

"A lot of people we talked to today were intimidated," Casey said as she sat across from them in the booth. "Nothing specific, but there's a lot of tension."

"We also need to find the ex-wife. I really think she has something to tell us."

"Not to change the subject, but...well, to change the subject, you're all set for the wedding now?"

After the turbulent day, this was something out of a different world.

"I think we are," Ellie said. "We have the date and the venue, a license, invitations out and dresses."

"You guys have a cake, too, right?" Casey asked, laughing when Jordan and Ellie gave her a blank look. "Oh my God. You know you can't get married without a cake, right?"

<hr />

They had spent part of the evening browsing websites of bakeries, but the next morning, any sweet delicacies were far from

Ellie's mind as she sat across from Ryan Lemont in the confines of the small room.

Waters stood sulking against the wall—though not far enough in Ellie's opinion. She could still feel him breathing down her neck. Lemont gave her a lazy grin. "Well, if it isn't Nancy Drew again."

"I'm surprised you have an appreciation for young adult literature. Good for you, but that's not why I'm here. You lied to me."

He laughed. "Honey, I lied to a lot of women. So what?"

"We have a pretty conclusive list of your high-profile clients. I guess it's true that you prefer them, but you wouldn't turn down a big chunk of the local market, would you?"

"I don't know what you're talking about. I'm thinking you don't know either."

Ellie leaned back in her chair, studying him—hoping he'd start to fidget at some point, that the authority she had in this situation would have more weight than appearances. She had to rely on that, because she had to ruefully admit that it would be hard otherwise to intimidate the drug dealer.

"Don't worry about that. I know a lot. I know you've had meetings with the neighborhood watch, which is kind of strange, since they promised they'd drive people like you out of town."

"People like me, isn't that some sort of bias? Can I sue for that?" he asked, still grinning.

"People in your business, Ryan. Getting drugs out on the streets and, wait, into schools. If someone gave you contacts to get it done and took care of the competition at the same time, that would be an offer too good to walk away from. I imagine you took it."

"Keep imagining," he scoffed, but there was a minute change to his demeanor. Ellie wasn't celebrating yet. She had come into the room with the plan to get him to say something compromising—for him, for Stanton—on the record.

"There are witnesses, Ryan, who saw you meet with Bob Stanton. What were you talking about in those meetings? The self-proclaimed law and order guy and the drug dealer, an odd couple, don't you think? I asked you the wrong question the last time. You weren't selling him drugs. He agreed to let you be and lean harder on all the others, and you…what did you do for him in return? Get rid of a homeless man who was bothering him?"

Lemont shook his head, exasperated.

"It will come out anyway, and the way it looks right now, both of you are going down. How hard, that's up to you. If you come clean now, we might even be able to help you."

Silence greeted her words. While Ellie had expected nothing else, she was still aware of the pressure. She needed something to take to Jarrod later. A bluff would perhaps do with the teenager, making him think that Lemont was going to turn on him and Stanton, but she would have loved to present something more substantial—to Jarrod, her colleagues, and the lieutenant.

"Look, we both know you're not new to this. You know how it works. You can talk to me now or wait until Bob and his friends get scared enough to talk, and when they do, that will be pretty bad for you. Your choice."

She pushed her chair back and got up.

"You'll be surprised. The guy's a freaking psychopath."

Ellie suppressed a smile, her heart beating faster.

"You know, not just any story to save your hide will do." She made a move to leave, only to hear his exaggerated sigh.

"I provide high quality entertainment to a lot of important people," he said. "Some of them might even be in your line of work. They're all adults, and they know what they're in for."

She slowly sat down again. "Even if I were to believe you, what's your point again?"

"I don't sell to kids. That's what I told them."

"Drugs, blackmail, murder, but you draw the line at selling in school, I see. That's noble of you...kind of."

"This is no joke. I've done some shit, yes, but I didn't kill the waitress. I don't know who did."

"What about Marco Raynor?"

"I don't know that either."

"Come on!" Ellie got to her feet again, this time walking straight to the door.

"I know there was a hit out for him. I didn't pay for it."

"Really?" It was the first time Waters spoke. "Then who did?"

"I have no idea. I could ask around, but...as it is, I'm stuck here, aren't I?"

Ellie cast a glance at her partner, wishing they had a rapport as easy as Jordan and Derek. She was pretty sure that part of what Lemont said was true, but that he was jerking them around at the same time. They needed to figure out which part was which, but she wasn't sure Waters would be helpful. At least, they had more people on the case now.

"Think hard. We'll be back later, and you better have some answers for us. Have a good day, Mr. Lemont."

Chapter Fifteen

W atching Ellie on the job was hard for Jordan, even though she knew she'd have to get over herself, and soon. The interrogation made her squirm with all sorts of unprofessional sentiments. She felt ever protective of Ellie, having to resist the urge to barge into the room at any sign of disrespect from either Waters or Lemont.

And then, seeing her make a seasoned criminal uneasy was just plain hot.

When they sat in Jordan's car to go to a diner nearby for lunch break, the greeting became a little more passionate than intended. Who could blame her? The wedding was weeks away. She was giddy and in love, and for once in her life, not waiting for the other shoe to drop.

"Okay. Hi," Ellie said, a content smile on her face. "I did okay, didn't I?"

"Hell, yes. I wish it was time to go home, then I could show you in more detail." Her frank words made Ellie blush, which did nothing to disperse her inappropriate emotions. A rap on the window made them both jump.

"Get a room, you two," Casey said after Jordan had rolled down the window. "You got a cake yet?"

"Keep this up and you won't be getting any," Jordan threatened her. Casey walked away laughing. "Okay, I don't have much time. Let's get something to eat."

Ellie leaned back in her seat with a sigh. "Yeah. I'm hungry, I guess."

"What's wrong?" Jordan asked as she pulled out of the parking lot. "I might be a bit biased, but I wasn't kidding. You did as well as anyone could have. You rattled him. I don't know that I believe he had nothing to do with the murders, but he gave us something to work with. That'll be helpful when you talk to that Jarrod guy."

"Yeah. Hopefully. Did you have any luck finding the ex yet?"

Jordan had spent part of her time since assigned to the case trying to find Stanton's ex.

"I have a last known address I'll check after lunch. I'll get back to you as soon as I can."

"Thank you. You know, I wouldn't mind some cake. Empty calories sound really good right now."

Jordan smiled, thinking they might tame her out of control emotions as well. "Sounds good to me."

Life couldn't get any better, could it? On top of it all, Kathryn hadn't called or texted in a while, obviously accepting that Jordan needed some distance between them on all levels.

❧

After lunch, they returned to the department. From there, Jordan went to check out the address of Bob Stanton's ex. Ellie and Waters went to see Jarrod Tanner.

Jarrod lived with his grandparents, and at the first sight of the police, he tried to run away, not getting any farther than Waters who was waiting for him at the back entrance.

He had his reasons, Ellie reflected as she stood in his room a moment later. If the neighborhood watch had ever started out with an innocent and righteous purpose, they sure had gone a long way from it. Judging from the flyers, books and paraphernalia on display, the group Jarrod Tanner was so proud to belong to looked more like far-right extremists.

"Don't jump to any conclusions yet," Waters mumbled.

"I'm not jumping to anything, don't worry."

Waters didn't say much else, both of them aware that some of his convictions slightly overlapped with the likes of Stanton and Tanner.

It should be a subject, Ellie thought. With the kind of power they were given in their jobs, questions should be asked whether they'd be able to approach everyone fairly. Officer Atwood's words came to mind. For every one of them, other cops had to work twice as hard to get the job done and earn the public's trust.

"This might all be concerning, but remember, we are looking for something illegal."

"Yeah. I'll keep that in mind."

The only person living at Sandy Beck's last known address was Sandy's former roommate, who reluctantly let Jordan in.

"It's no secret," she said. "Sandy moved out after she got her feet back under her, and she remarried."

"She ever talked to you about why she didn't appear in court that time?"

"She just wanted to put a terrible relationship behind her, not ever see him again. I don't think you can blame her."

"Do you think Bob Stanton threatened her?"

"Think?" the woman scoffed. "He called her several times a day and showed up here too. Sometimes bringing flowers, sometimes telling her that if he couldn't have her, no one would."

"Did she report these threats?"

Jordan knew the answer already. After the initial charges that were filed and dropped, Sandy had never contacted the police again.

"What good would that do? She left, and that was the best idea. She has a new life now. I hope you don't have to bother her and bring it all up again."

"I hope so too. Did you or Sandy know about the dealings of Bob's neighborhood watch?"

"There was a lot of posturing, I remember. I don't know if they actually did everything they said, but there was always talk about how some people are draining society. The usual suspects, you get the picture. Bob especially had it in for some homeless guy hanging out at the park."

"You know his name?"

"No, but he was young. Asked people for a dollar every once in a while, but he always walked away when they said no. Bob, he was really thrilled when those college kids killed the homeless woman, said they'd done us all a favor. Freaky."

"Yeah. Thank you for your time, I appreciate it."

The picture was getting clearer by the minute. Jordan remembered that even Lemont had called Stanton a psychopath, which was quite the label to be given by a career criminal. Ellie had been on to something right from the start.

She hoped to catch her before she got to interview Jarrod Tanner.

"I know my rights," Tanner exclaimed. He looked nervous. Chances were he knew that the odds were stacked against him, that both Stanton and Lemont would see him as expendable.

"Yeah, don't worry about that. You'd like to call your lawyer?"

"You'll let me have my call?" he asked, suspicious.

"Sure, as you say, it's your right. You have a lawyer, right? It makes sense given the company you keep."

"You have to get me one if I can't afford it, right?"

Ellie exchanged a smile with Derek Henderson, glad to have him with her in the room instead of Waters who had left without giving her details.

"You haven't been arrested or charged with anything," she clarified. "Running from the police, it looks a little suspicious, but I'm sure we can clear all of that up. Right now, we're just talking."

"What if I don't want to talk? What is this anyway, good cop/bad cop? Or minority cops deciding the white guy must be guilty anyway?"

"Whoa, Jarrod, slow down. No one's deciding anything right now."

Ellie wished she could roll her eyes, but even so, she assumed she and Derek were thinking the same at this moment.

"To get this out of the way, you're a member of Stanton's neighborhood watch."

"That's right. I'm proud of it."

"And you also took part in one of your university programs, on how to help the homeless?"

She hadn't quite managed to keep the disbelief out of her voice, Ellie could tell from his expression.

"Yeah, so? I thought it came with some goals, but there was a lot of talking and bleeding hearts."

"With some exceptions," Ellie reminded him. "There was someone in the group who thought differently."

"I never even talked to them. Anyway, the work that Bob's guys do is a lot more effective. We protect hard-working citizens."

"All right...Then again, people are telling us that this neighborhood watch business is getting out of hand. You are aware that Lemont was arrested and charged with murder. The same guy you and Bob Stanton met with. We want to know why."

"Why? To tell him to get lost, of course. That was the whole point."

"Really? He tells a different story," Derek stated.

Jarrod stared at him morosely.

"Then he's lying. He's a fucking drug dealer. You figure it out."

"The story we're hearing," Ellie continued, "is that Stanton and Lemont needed you to get the drugs into your school. There's nothing to it, then? Because, sure, it's bad, but murder is worse. If you can tell us anything that will help, we might cut you some slack on the dealing."

"I didn't do anything. You just don't like me because I have traditional values. Deal with it."

Derek coughed.

"I guess I have to remind you, this has nothing to do with values. It's about homicide."

"I thought you said Lemont was charged offing that slut? Not like he does things himself."

"I'm not talking about Rena Kelly." That moment, Ellie needed to say the woman's name. With some satisfaction, she noticed the red splotches appearing on Jarrod's face. So it had an effect on him too. "Marco Raynor."

"Never heard of him."

"You guys have been hanging out at Patton Lake Park a lot. Bob had a problem with Marco in particular."

"Hey, can you blame him? I go to school and work. They do nothing all day and harass the tourists for money, and the police coddle them."

"So, you decided to teach him a lesson?"

"I didn't."

"But your friend Bob did? Look, perhaps it's time for you to think of your options here. We've heard from several people now, and it doesn't look like he cares much about anyone but himself."

"You said you're not charging me with anything."

"Well, son, that could change the moment Lemont or Stanton decide they want to save their hides," Derek reminded him. "You admire Bob so much you are ready to be the fall guy for him?"

"I'm not your son."

Ellie caught Derek's glance, indicating that he was quite happy about that fact.

"That's the only thing you're taking away from this?" she asked. "You could be going to prison for a long time."

He looked Ellie up and down, but she could tell there were cracks in the cocky façade.

"I think I want my lawyer now," he said.

"You don't need a lawyer. You're free to go."

⁂

Ellie had retreated to the break room with Derek, needing a fix of caffeine and sugar.

"I'm not sure Cliff or Lieutenant Carroll will be satisfied with that," she said ruefully. At least the hot coffee and the chocolate bar helped—some. She wondered if she was cut out for this work after all. She had watched Derek and Jordan many times. They were an experienced team, and they always seemed to catch the suspect's weakness.

"Well, Cliff should have shown up if he wanted a different result. You're going for the right strategy," he assured her. "This will cause some ripples. One of them will crack."

"Yeah, but we don't know that for sure. I hate to admit it, but this is harder than it looks."

"Come on, you are doing better than okay. You got information out of Raphael Deane that no one else had. You built a rapport with Raynor that helped us."

"And they're both dead now." Ellie winced. That wasn't what she'd meant to say. "I guess I have to rely on appearing harmless."

"You'll have to be the good cop for the time being," Derek agreed good-naturedly. "Ellie, that's not a bad thing. We all use the skills we have to our advantage. No two suspects are the same. We have to be flexible as well."

"I'm not sure if that's consoling me but thank you."

"You go with what works."

"Yeah. I'll remember that."

Painting a picture was not enough though. They needed something to bring in Stanton, and so far, that goal hadn't come closer into reach.

Chapter Sixteen

Since Ellie and Derek were still occupied with exploring the neighborhood watch, it was Maria who met Jordan at the crime scene, the parking lot of a closed furniture factory on the edge of the area where grey buildings and concrete slowly gave way to better kept buildings and tourist condos.

The dead man was white, mid-thirties, one shot to the head. There was no ID on him, but eight twenty-dollar bills rolled and wedged into his back pocket.

"He made someone angry," Maria commented.

"That is for sure. And I'd venture to say he saw it coming," ME Melissa Adams added. "Look."

Peering at the bullet wound, Jordan saw a ringed bruise around the small hole. It looked like the perpetrator had pressed the gun against the man's forehead. At a range this close, blood must have spattered all over the shooter. Maybe they were lucky, and he hadn't gotten far. Uniformed officers were canvassing the neighborhood. She reached out with a gloved hand, pushing up the dead man's sleeve, finding what she was looking for—another bruise, circling his lower arm. This was why he hadn't run. There had been more than one person around. Perhaps the victim had even voluntarily met them. Had they given him the money? A deal gone bad? In any case, the perpetrators didn't seem to care much about $160.

There was no watch or any kind of jewelry, but the man's clothes and shoes looked new.

She walked to the edge of the parking lot, thinking this murder had to be well planned out. The looming buildings obstructed any view from nearby apartment complexes. The victim had probably walked into the situation oblivious, not expecting the people he was going to meet to do him any harm.

Jordan had read all the transcripts regarding Lemont and the neighborhood watch. In his first interview, he had claimed only to cater to a well-off clientele. This was his turf, and even though he was in prison, there was bound to be a number two taking care of what was left of his business.

She stepped off the curb, looking down the street to see a familiar sign in the distance: The bar where waitress Rena Kelly had worked. She'd been stabbed, found in the back room. All employees and the manager and owner had been cleared, since all traces, including DNA, had led to Lemont. They had witnesses placing him at the scene that night, and he'd obviously been cheating on Ashley.

Another murder in such close vicinity, in an area that Lemont had previously controlled, it couldn't be a coincidence.

If only Rena Kelly could talk.

It might be worth going back to the bar when it opened later and talk to employees and patrons again. There had to be a connection—and once they found it, perhaps the murder of Marco Raynor, and Bob Stanton's involvement would become clearer again.

⁂

Ellie and Derek weren't lucky with their planned follow-up on Bob Stanton. At the Stantons' house, his mother opened the front door, peering at them with suspicion.

"My son is not here. What do you want?"

"Ma'am, can you tell us where he is?"

"Why, he's done nothing wrong. Why do you keep bothering him?"

"It's important that we talk to him. He might have some information for us," Ellie tried to placate the woman. "It would be very helpful if—"

"He's visiting family," Stanton's mother cut her off. "If you want to talk to him, you'll have to wait until Monday."

"Thanks anyway," Derek mumbled, after the door fell shut nearly in their faces. "Let's head back and throw everything against the wall. Something's got to stick."

Ellie envied him his boundless enthusiasm, but she didn't say that out loud.

"I hope so. We have a cake tasting coming up."

Everyone had gathered in the briefing room to put together their respective pieces of the investigation, hoping to get closer to the complete picture.

Jordan had pushed back the time of the cake tasting they had scheduled. Now she stood in front of the board showing all the bits and pieces of the case.

"According to her colleague, Rena Kelly always locked at the end of her shift, left through the back door and went home on her bike. She normally would have taken this way..." She showed Kelly's usual commute on the map pinned to the board. "But there had been construction for a week or so, and she went by the park instead. We didn't pay much attention to that at the time because she was killed at the bar. Now I wonder if it's relevant that she took this other route."

"Including the night Marco Raynor was murdered," Ellie injected.

Waters sat next to her, looking bored. He hadn't given her any explanations as to his whereabouts in the past hours but told her he'd be taking some personal time to sell his condo. That was probably the most he had talked to her since the beginning of their partnership.

"Exactly. We don't know if she saw something, or if this is unrelated, but here's a theory—Stanton wants Raynor gone, and he makes a deal with the devil. When there's a witness implicating Lemont or one of his people, the devil comes to collect."

"But wasn't Lemont in a relationship with Rena Kelly?"

"We don't know that for sure. He knew her, hung out at the bar, and perhaps harassed her. I'd hardly call that a relationship."

Ellie nodded. "Yet, they are all closely connected in some way. Any luck on ID'ing John Doe yet?"

"Harry Travis. He's in the system," Maria Doss revealed. "Some drug offenses, did a little time, but lately he'd improved his legal representation. And get this, the guys who got him out the last time are familiar. We know of a few cases related to Lemont's crew."

"So what made them turn on him?" Ellie asked.

"We're going to find out. Who of you wants to spend tonight at one of the worst dives in town? Let's hope the health benefits cover that, too."

❧

"You again."

The manager of the bar where Rena Kelly had worked obviously recognized Jordan. He wasn't pleased to have the police in the house again.

"What are you doing here? I thought you got the drug dealer for the murder."

"Well, yeah, there are always others. Sorry for the inconvenience." He snorted but held up his hands in mock surrender.

"What is it this time? You know I told you everything. Life is better if people like Ryan Lemont aren't breathing down my neck."

"I'd think so, and we want to keep it that way, right? You've seen this guy before?"

He cast a cursory glance at the picture, wincing at the obvious cause of death. "Can't say I have."

"The name Harry Travis ring a bell?"

"Not to me, but please, try not to bother my people too much. They're working here."

"Yeah, so am I. You'd think I'd come here if I wasn't? Not really my scene."

"Then why don't you stay away, Detective?"

"Easy. I'm thinking the health department hasn't visited in a while, or am I wrong?"

His face reddened. "Do what you have to do, and then get lost."

"That's the plan."

◆

Ellie had been observing closely, studying Jordan's interaction with the manager, wondering what she could learn from it—or if she should go with Derek's theory for now, that appearing cute and harmless, still, would be to her benefit. At the moment, all it did for her was having to ward off advances and wandering hands. Jordan hadn't been kidding when she warned them about this place. She felt horrible thinking about Rena Kelly who had to work here, only to end up stabbed to death in the back room.

She forced the images from her mind and continued to mingle unobtrusively with staff and guests, looking for anyone who might have seen Travis. Most of the time, she got a quick denial. Ellie found it remarkable that no one seemed to be shocked much at being shown the image of a dead man.

"Miss? Can we go talk someone else?"

The soft whisper had come from the young woman who was vigorously wiping the table without looking up. Given that she might have important information, Ellie cut the woman some slack for calling her "miss."

"You have seen Mr. Travis?" she confirmed.

"Not here. My shift is over. Meet me out in the back in a couple of minutes."

She picked up the rag and turned abruptly for the counter.

Ellie looked around, but none of her colleagues were to be seen in the packed bar.

⚬⚬⚬

The crowd was as reluctant to talk to the police as they remembered from earlier visits, but they still managed to produce some results.

"He was definitely here a few times," Jordan summed up their findings. "That's something. I don't think we'll get more out of the people here. You guys want to join us for something to eat?"

"Sure." Derek winced. "After taking a bath in hand sanitizer, right? Yikes."

Jordan couldn't argue with him. "It hasn't changed, no doubt. You want to call Kate?"

"Yeah, let's call it a night."

"Where's Ellie?"

He shrugged. "No idea. I haven't seen her since we came here."

Jordan looked around the crowd. "I'll text her. The *D&T*, later?"

"Sure, let's do it."

She sent a quick text and then spotted Maria Doss talking to another patron.

"Hey, honey, want to dance?"

She quickly removed the hand from her backside. Her glare and the grip around his wrist obviously were enough for the man to get the message, but not before calling her frigid, and worse.

Jordan shook her head to herself and went to join Maria. Still no message from Ellie.

Maria hadn't seen her either, and the uneasy feeling in the pit of Jordan's stomach intensified rapidly. "Let's find her," she said.

⁂

"I want protection," the young woman said, nervously lighting a cigarette, as she and Ellie stood outside at the back of the building. "Can you do that?"

"That depends on what you are going to tell me. If you are in danger, we will help you."

"You better. I don't want to get killed, like Rena."

Ellie kept Jordan's earlier summary in mind. "You told the police that Rena had been taking a detour the past few days before she was killed. Do you think she saw anything?"

"I know she did. She told me."

"Rena witnessed the murder?"

"I don't know! She said they were fighting, beating up one of the homeless people in the park. Since she had heard about some having been killed before, she ran. That's all I know."

"She ever mentioned someone named Harry Travis?"

"Not to me."

"You saw him here at the bar?"

The woman's eyes widened when she looked at the picture. "That's not his name when he's here, and you bet I saw him. He came to see Rena a few times."

At this point, Ellie couldn't help feeling frustrated. Too many detours and diversions, and omissions that could have helped them move forward.

"Why didn't you ever mention him?"

"No one asked me about him. Everyone thought it was Ryan who killed her, well, I thought that too. Rena didn't want to be just the mistress, and well, he didn't like anyone talking back to him. Do you think someone else might have done it?"

"We don't know yet. But I'd like you to come to the station with me and make a statement. Don't worry. We'll make sure no one knows."

"No one knows what?" Jordan asked, and she didn't sound amused.

"I know, right? I'm sorry. I was in the middle of something there. I know it's not much, but..."

"It's something." Jordan finally softened her stance somewhat. "Someone thought Rena could identify them, and either Travis or Lemont took care of it. Lemont's involved either way, but it might be Travis who actually killed her. Then they took care of that loose end too. Now if only we knew what they saw, it might all unravel and not look good for Bob Stanton and his guys."

"It's still all theory," Ellie sighed as they sat over pizza and wine, much later that evening, not yet ready to set the workday aside for a moment.

"It's coming together."

"You were worried about me." It wasn't a question.

"Considering all that happened in that place, can you blame me? I know you can take care of yourself. I also know I had half a dozen patrons grabbing my ass or trying to. It wouldn't be a loss to anyone if the city shut down that joint."

"I don't blame you. I agree." Ellie leaned back in the booth. "It's just going so slow. I mean we know Stanton is an ass who beats up and intimidates women, and we're pretty sure he had a bit of drug trade going on the side. Yet, we can't bust him until we prove the latter without a doubt, and that could take forever."

"Welcome to detective work. The lucky breaks are few and far between," Jordan supplied helpfully. "Tomorrow, we need to do that cake tasting by the way. If we actually want to have a cake for the day."

"That should be okay. At least the dresses are all ready to go."

"They made a few changes to mine," Jordan admitted, blushing a bit.

"Oh, really?" Ellie couldn't imagine what those would be.

"Yes, really. I'll go back to the gym a little more often after the wedding, so for now, they won't have to change it back...That was a bit startling. Don't laugh."

"I'm not laughing." She might not have been able to hide the smile soon enough. It was hard enough to get Jordan to eat breakfast on a regular basis, and there as no doubt she had been under a lot of stress lately. Ellie tended to reward herself when that happened. Jordan mostly did the opposite. "You could use that couple of pounds."

"Well, good, I have some to spare." Maria Doss slid into the booth. "Also, I was hearing cake which might be the best thing of the day."

That, they could all agree on.

Chapter Seventeen

B y the time Bob Stanton was due to return from his family trip, Dr. Melissa Adams had done the autopsy on Harry Travis, a man of medium health and not so many secrets. The bullet that had killed him came from the same gun as the one that had killed Marco Raynor.

That morning, Ryan Lemont's lawyer signaled that his client was interested in a deal.

Ellie and Waters met with A.D.A. Esposito before the scheduled meeting.

"He better help us unravel this mess completely," she said, "before we give him anything. If he didn't stab Rena Kelly, he hired someone else to do so, likely Travis, before he got him killed too. I can offer him a few years off the sentence, but that's it."

"Not sure his lawyer will go with that," Waters returned.

Ellie could only describe Esposito's look at him as a glare.

"I do my work based on what you give me, so the better you do your job, the less leeway I need to give lowlife like that," she said.

Ellie did her best to make herself look invisible.

"Well, at least we have something, thanks to Harding." Esposito sighed. "Let's see what Lemont has. If it's not anything big in the first ten minutes, I'm out of there."

"Thank you," Ellie mumbled, slightly in awe of the woman's strict, confident demeanor, until she remembered again that Valerie was an ex of Jordan's. Talk about a dilemma. For now, though, Esposito was right—they had to do their jobs, nothing else.

"Well, if it isn't Nancy Drew again," Lemont greeted her. His lawyer, Ellie could tell, barely refrained himself from rolling his eyes. He didn't, of course. In the kind of hierarchy he was working in, disobedience could get a person killed. In the case of Harry Travis, even doing everything by the boss's book could get someone killed, so she could understand the attorney keeping his emotions in check.

"You wanted to meet," Waters reminded him. Even if Ellie had prodded and insisted, and it was basically due to her that more people were working these connected cases now, the more experienced detective was taking charge. She had expected it but couldn't help being slightly disappointed.

"Well, yeah, I don't get to see so many good-looking chicks on the inside."

He winked at Esposito who shook her head and got up.

"Forget about it. This is a waste of time."

"Hey, wait. Lady. Listen. We both know that I'm no choirboy."

Valerie Esposito had no reservations. She did roll her eyes. "If that's all you have to say, the meeting is over."

"I didn't kill Rena. I know who might have."

"Well, so do we." Ellie couldn't help it. "Harry Travis is on a slab in the morgue. You don't like witnesses. We know that too."

"Oh come on, Harry ran into trouble all by himself. I thought the gentleman next to me would be doing a better job so we wouldn't need to have this conversation, but here we are." The lawyer looked positively scared now. "You know I met with those bums that patrol the neighborhood. I told you I wasn't going to do business with them, and I wasn't. That would cast a bad light on my clients."

"Sure."

No one in the room had missed the biting sarcasm in Esposito's one word.

"You, unfortunately, saw the list. There's no need to be condescending. We all need to make a living, right?"

"Focus, Mr. Lemont."

He was still wearing a smile, but Ellie could have sworn she saw a flash of fury on his face. He might deny close associations with Stanton, but they were cut from the same cloth, despising women with authority.

"Can you imagine? They were trying to blackmail me. A guy with a beer gut and a pimply teenager threatening to run me off. You know I have honest business in this city, right? They had a point though—some of those bums at Patton Lake were getting awfully chummy with the police, and some of them might have been rats. That meeting wasn't about drugs, but I agreed that if they wanted to clean up the park, my guys would stay out of it. Stanton came by one time to ask for a favor in exchange for some things he knew. I told Harry to escort him out, and next thing I knew I'm charged with the murder of that waitress. I guess I was just putting it together as you did."

"And you know nothing about what was said between the two of them?"

He shook his head. "Would I lie to you?" Ryan Lemont didn't wait for the obvious answer. "My ass is on the line, all right? I trusted Harry, but he got himself into some shit—sorry, Ladies—that caught up with him."

"I'd feel better if you had something concrete to give us. I fail to see how this helps our investigation."

"Wait, I'm not done. There's a knife that exchanged hands somewhere in that meeting. I saw the two of them together. I asked Harry about it, but he said it was nothing, something Beer Gut had borrowed from him. Wait, did I mention the two of them were cousins? Stanton once asked him to be part of his posse, but Harry had higher aspirations."

"Like working for you, or murder—or both?"

"I'd say he made a fine choice working for me. The rest is for you to figure out, but perhaps you can find the bloody knife at Stanton's house. So what am I getting out of this?"

"We'll see if your story checks out," Esposito said. "Then we'll talk again."

"Hey! You'll solve two murders because of me, who do you think offed the homeless guy? Doing each other favors, and then Stanton tried to clean up the mess like an amateur."

"Yeah, sure, we'll talk later."

"Don't dismiss me like that!" Lemont jumped to his feet, rattling his cuffs so abruptly the guard stepped closer to him. "Do you really think that if I had him killed, it would be with the same gun? I'm not that stupid. Are you?"

"We're done here," Esposito said tersely. "Time for Mr. Stanton to answer some questions."

❦

"Whatever place he had on the totem pole, I can't imagine anyone associated with Lemont would do anything without his okay," Ellie surmised, glad it was Derek with her once more while Waters was supposedly taking care of his condo.

Jordan had watched the interrogation, and she had stayed behind for some follow-up with Valerie Esposito. Ellie suppressed a sigh. Things were happening in this case, finally. She had no reason to worry about Valerie otherwise, with the wedding less than a month away.

"You're right. It will be hard to prove though."

"Yeah. Those closest to him are either scared or dead."

They arrived at Stanton's house only to find his mother glaring at them once again. "Bob isn't here yet. He called me to say he took a later plane."

"Did he say why?" Derek asked.

"No, he just left a voicemail. He doesn't have to justify himself, right? You're trespassing, unless you have a warrant."

"Actually, Ma'am," Ellie said, "you're wrong on both. It's extremely important that we speak to your son. And," she held out the paper for Mrs. Stanton to see, "we'd like to take a look around."

"So, how are you doing?" Valerie asked when the official part was over.

Jordan busied herself finishing up her notes.

"Fine," she said. "Perfect. Why are you asking?"

"Oh, I don't know. Granted, things were fairly superficial between us, but that doesn't mean I don't care, right? With your biological mother helping out on a case, and the wedding around the corner, I can only imagine you're freaking out about things too good to be true."

Jordan wondered if it was rude to tell Valerie flat out this was none of her business. Rude, possibly, true, as well. She also wondered if she was really that predictable.

"It's been challenging," she acknowledged. "Still great. The wedding part, I mean. I'm sorry we didn't invite you, but that would have been…"

"Slightly awkward, I get it."

"I'm glad you do, but it's not just that. We are trying to keep it small."

"Yeah, sure, I understand. Anyway, good for you. Harding is making herself at home too, I see. I'm happy for you both."

"Thanks."

"You're welcome. Now get back to work. I'd love to file some charges that stick by the end of the day."

"Will do, Ma'am." Jordan made a faux salute and was finally able to leave the office.

She stopped to greet Mindy, Valerie's secretary, who was behind her desk.

On her way out, she nearly ran into a man who gave her an angry glare.

"Excuse me," she mumbled with a shrug, looking back over her shoulder as he strode past her. She was on the other side of the door, a few steps into the hallway, when she heard Mindy call, "Sir, you can't go in there. Sir—" –and then a scream, as a shot rang out, and then another.

Jordan drew her weapon and went back inside, gesturing to a terrified looking Mindy to get out.

❦

Ellie let Derek do most of the search—as for any hints of Stanton's whereabouts they certainly would be back later. She sat down with Mrs. Stanton in the living room while Derek continued upstairs, hoping to forge some sort of rapport with the woman and keep her from warning her son.

"Listen, I know it must be unsettling to have the police come in like this."

"Barging in is more like it."

180

"I know," Ellie said, even though that wasn't the truth. "I know you don't want us here, but your son got involved with some very dangerous people. He might be a witness to a crime, and those people have a lot to lose."

"Are you threatening me and my son?" Mrs. Stanton demanded, indignantly. She seemed hell-bent on misinterpreting Ellie. "He is only trying to help his neighbors, but these days, if you do that, you're the bad person, while others get away with everything."

"I am not threatening anyone. You can help Bob now if you tell us where he is."

"I told you, he took a later plane."

"Can you play me that message?"

"No. I deleted it. I didn't know you'd need it."

"Mrs. Stanton, do you know for sure that Bob has left town?"

"You're accusing him of lying?"

"I don't know. Maybe he got scared. If he talks to the police now, we can help him."

The woman gave her a dubious look, and for the umpteenth time, Ellie wished she'd look older, or anything that would make people take her more at her word.

"I can't tell you what to believe," she finally said. "But one thing's for sure. Every minute that Bob doesn't turn himself in, it will look worse for him."

Her phone vibrated, indicating an incoming text message.

"Excuse me."

Ellie had barely skimmed over the words on the screen when she jumped to her feet. She took a card out of her pocket and handed it to a reluctant Mrs. Stanton.

"I'm sorry, but we need to go. If you hear from Bob, call us right away. You're doing the right thing for him. Someone has to if he won't do it."

She heard Derek coming down the stairs before he joined them in the living room, his gaze serious.

"Ellie, you should come see this."

"I don't think we have the time."

There was another message, and Ellie's stomach lurched before she opened it.

Chapter Eighteen

W hen she entered Valerie's office, Jordan was grateful to find the situation almost under control. The man she'd just run into was writhing on the floor, clutching his thigh.

Valerie held a gun in shaking hands, hers, Jordan assumed. She spotted the intruder's at a fairly safe distance.

"Show me your hands, asshole," she snapped at him.

"I can't. I'm bleeding," he whined.

"Oh, you can. Move it. Now."

"I need a doctor."

"Yeah, I can see that. I don't think the A.D.A. appreciates you bleeding all over her carpet."

She phoned security first, as she assumed a possible lockdown was only moments away. "This is Detective Carpenter. I'm in A.D.A. Esposito's office. We're okay. The intruder is alive, but he'll need medical assistance." Her words brought on an undignified yelp. "Could you please get a medic in here ASAP?" On second thought, Valerie might need one too. Jordan noticed that she hadn't moved.

"Hey, Val," she said softly after hanging up with the security guard. "You're okay?" She couldn't blame her for being shell-shocked. Having to defend herself against an armed intruder in her own office was definitely not part of the job description.

"You can lay down the gun now. Careful. Sit. He's not going anywhere."

Simple reassurances seemed to work, and with the perpetrator cuffed, Jordan took a deep breath. Crisis averted.

After the security guards and the paramedics, Maria and Waters were first to arrive with a couple of uniforms. Chris Atwood looked fairly excited to be in the midst of this situation—*figures*, Jordan thought, irritated. Libby Marshall, a friend of Ellie and Kate's, was also with them,

Jordan longed to call Ellie. She had certainly heard of the incident by now. Jordan didn't want her to worry.

She looked over to where Maria was talking to Valerie, asking her to come over for a statement once the paramedic was done checking on her.

"I'll take her," Jordan said.

Waters made a face. "Someone will interview you as well, as you're in the middle of this mess as usual."

"Yeah, thanks for the lecture, I'm aware," she said, running out of patience with her colleague. To Maria, she continued, "It's going to take all day anyway. How about I'll get her a coffee first, and you let me know when you're ready to get started?"

"Works for me," Maria said, the easy interaction causing their two male co-workers to bristle. Jordan missed Derek, but apparently, until Waters was retired and Atwood off to another precinct, everyone had to draw the short straw sometime.

"Thank you," Valerie whispered when they were last to leave the office save for the CSU crew. "The crazy thing is I'm not even sure what happened. He came in, I saw he had a gun, and I just reacted."

"It's a good thing you did."

Jordan didn't think it was a good moment to mention all the other things that could have happened or ask Valerie why she kept a gun in her drawer. Superficial, it was true, their relationship had been like that. She didn't know her all that well. If people knew, or thought they knew, a lot more about Jordan, it was only because a lot of cases had hit too close too home in the past.

They walked along the walkway connecting their buildings, and Jordan quickly ushered Valerie into the break room before anyone could want to start a conversation. Ryan Lemont's interrogation seemed like forever ago—even though it wasn't. Watching, she had seen the anger in his face at some things Valerie had said, but he didn't have the time or opportunity to get the word out...or did he?

When Valerie sat in one of the chairs, she turned to the vending machine and got them both coffees and snacks. Waters had been right in one thing: An endless number of interviews would follow, with an incident right here at the A.D.A.'s workplace, and a cop on the periphery.

Jordan put everything on the table, only to realize that Valerie was crying.

"It's okay. That really sucked," she said, laying a hand on her shoulder, ever awkward in the presence of unexpected emotion.

◦◦◦

"We need to go back. There's been a shooting at the D.A.'s office," Ellie told Derek in a whisper. His eyes widened.

"Did anyone get hurt?"

"It doesn't sound like it. They got the guy, but...Jordan was with A.D.A. Esposito. I need to check on her."

Derek took the phone from her and read over the text message. "She's okay," he said firmly. "You really need to see this."

Ellie appreciated his attempt at helping her to keep focus. All she wanted was to see Jordan. She felt light-headed with relief that no one, especially not Jordan, got hurt, but she needed to see for herself.

"I'll take a look and then we go."

"Of course."

On the upper floor, they found a whole room dedicated to hunting trophies and paraphernalia.

"Knives," Ellie said. "Like the one he gave Travis?"

"There was a break-in recently."

Both of them jumped at the voice of Mrs. Stanton behind them. "They stole several knives."

"Why didn't he report it to the police?" Derek asked.

She laughed bitterly. "Seeing how the police treated him, like a suspect, like he was no better than those bums in the park, I can't see why."

"Can you tell us where this was taken?" Derek, unfazed, pointed to a framed photograph on the wall. Ellie noticed that Jarrod Tanner was among the six men in the picture, a teenager at the time.

To their surprise, Mrs. Stanton had an answer for them.

"I'm not sure, but it might be Jarrod's cabin. The kid inherited it after his grandfather died."

"Do you have an address?" Ellie asked.

"No. You'll have to ask him."

All of a sudden, it didn't look like they were going back to the station anytime soon. Derek asked for backup, and they were on their way to meet Jarrod Tanner on his college campus.

❦

I can't come back right now. Are you okay? Ellie texted and got an answer right away.

Fine. Don't worry. Cake tasting off again?

I'm afraid so. On the way to Tanner's. Can I see you for a sec?

Derek good-naturedly rolled his eyes when he caught a glimpse of Ellie opening the video chat screen. He was all show, Ellie knew, just as relieved that Jordan was okay. She sighed in relief when Jordan appeared on the screen.

"I don't have much time," she said. "Val and I snuck away for some coffee and chocolate in the break room, but they're ready to interview us now."

These were extraordinary circumstances, so Ellie wouldn't fret about the obvious familiarity. "How is she?"

"As good as can be expected when someone walks into their office and pulls a gun. It's hitting her now, but she'll be fine."

"And you?" Ellie asked, feeling like Jordan was stalling on her behalf.

"I'm good, I promise. She had shot the guy and kicked away the gun when I came in."

Still too close for her comfort, but Ellie didn't say that.

"We might know where to find Stanton. I'll see you later then."

"Yeah. Be careful," Jordan advised as if she hadn't just been in a situation with an active shooter. Ellie didn't waste time arguing.

"Always. I love you."

"Love you too. Bye."

"Bye," Ellie said before ending the call, and to Derek, "Don't say a word."

"I'm not saying anything. Love is great."

It truly was, but now it was time to switch gears and find Bob Stanton before he could harm anyone else.

❧

An attack on an Assistant District Attorney raised many questions. It could be as easy as the latest case she was prosecuting or something much bigger. Jordan wasn't surprised when the woman conducting her interview introduced herself as the lieutenant of Major Crimes. Jordan had heard that she'd started in the job recently, so she hadn't met her before. It was possible that even the FBI would look into this, depending on what they uncovered about the shooter's intentions and background.

She was glad she'd had the foresight to get some caffeine and sugar while she could. It wasn't the same as exclusive cakes and coffee specialties they might have had at the tasting. For now, it had to do.

"I was going over notes from an interview with A.D.A. Esposito. I was just leaving her office when I saw him coming in. I heard the secretary say something to him, because he apparently walked straight past her. I was on the other sight of the door then," Jordan explained what seemed to be one of many times.

"You didn't recognize the man at all?"

"No. The way he was dressed he could have had an appointment. Of course, when I heard the gunshots, it was clear to me that he didn't."

"Two gunshots, you said."

"Exactly. I think he fired one shot, missed, and the other shot came from A.D.A. Esposito's gun."

"We'll figure that out, thank you," the lieutenant said. "For now, let's stick to what you actually saw."

"No problem." Jordan refrained from sighing or mentioning that she had repeated what little she knew for a few times now. "I came in, saw the intruder on the floor. He was injured. I could arrest him and notify security that the situation was under control."

"Detective Carpenter, why didn't you call for backup first?"

Jordan wasn't amused, mostly, because this was a somewhat legit question, and she was going to hear about it, from her own lieutenant, from Ellie, and perhaps a few other people.

"There was no time? I thought this was about figuring out why someone would want to shoot the A.D.A. We were interrogating Ryan Lemont again this morning. He doesn't deal well with women ordering him around, so perhaps that's where you should be looking. You're welcome." At the lieutenant's expression, she sat up straighter. "I'm sorry about that. No offense."

"None taken," the woman assured her. "Perhaps we should take a break here?"

"I'd rather continue if that means I can go home sometime today."

You don't know it, but if all goes well, I could still make it to that cake tasting.

"In that case, let me get some more coffee in here. If you'll excuse me for a moment."

"I'll take mine with milk," Jordan called after her, even though she rarely did.

⚭

"Yes, that was at my grandfather's cabin," Tanner confirmed. "The guys took me hunting with them. There was nothing illegal about it."

"We're not saying that," Ellie clarified, impatient. "We need the address, now."

"What's the hurry?"

"Mr. Tanner, please?"

"I don't know what you think you could find there," he said, scribbling it on a notepad, "but here it is. I guess you have a warrant, but this is my key, just so you don't break down the door. Don't make a mess like they always do on TV, okay?"

"No mess. Got it."

The sarcasm in Derek's tone had gone completely over the young man's head.

"Good. If that's all? I have to go back to class now."

When they were back in the car, Ellie voiced her thoughts. "I didn't expect him to be this cooperative. I hope that doesn't mean there's a bad surprise waiting for us."

Derek didn't argue. Perhaps he'd had the same thought.

❦

This coffee didn't come from a vending machine. It was a latte, actually, making Jordan slightly suspicious. Did the lieutenant think she needed to soften her up a bit?

"That's good. Thank you."

"You're welcome, Detective. Now, I do have another question. Did you know A.D.A. Esposito kept a gun in her office?"

"No." There was nothing more to it.

"Your relationship is merely professional, or you're...friends?"

"Those are a lot more than one question. Okay. Yeah, I guess you could say we're friends. Not close friends, obviously, but putting away bad guys is a uniting factor." Jordan didn't think it was necessary to share something that should have never happened in the first place—she and Valerie agreed on that these days. Valerie, too, would certainly understand the meaning behind this line of questioning, so she was unlikely to bring it up herself. "I know that you have to cover all the bases, but I can save you some time here. Yes, the A.D.A. was very lucky to be able to react the way she did. It was a coincidence that I was there, but if you want my opinion, it's likely to do with one of her cases, possibly Lemont. Since the neighborhood watch has been driving out the smaller players, there are a lot more folks that answer to him."

"Thanks for the theory, Detective." The woman was good, not a hint of sarcasm in her voice. "I was thinking of it myself, then again, the A.D.A. says something this morning that pisses him off, he snaps his fingers, and a guy with a gun walks in? That easy?"

"She's ready to put him away for a long time," Jordan said. "He ought to have been pissed off for a while now."

"I heard something about a new suspect in the Rena Kelly case."

"That changes very little. It was still Ryan Lemont who was pulling the strings to have her killed."

"You're sure about that? Because if that case starts falling apart, not only it would be questionable if you could still hold him. He might be suing you."

"He wanted Kelly dead. She is dead. That's all I can tell you."

Jordan shook her head in disbelief. Did anyone really think Valerie would come up with an elaborate scheme because she didn't have enough to prosecute Lemont? To call this a reach would be mild.

"No need to get defensive," the other woman chided her. "Believe me, we know how important it is to make those charges stick. This attack is reprehensible, and we want to make sure the right people will be held accountable. Thanks for your time, Detective. We'll be in touch."

"I understand," Jordan said before she shook the woman's hand and left the room.

She wanted to find out what they had asked Valerie, and how she was doing. She was also interested in what they'd learned from the shooter.

Most of all, Jordan wanted to know where Ellie's investigation had led her, but since there was no message from either her or Derek, she assumed they were busy.

Maria and Waters were at their respective desks. They, too, were waiting for news from the other team.

❦

"Police! We're coming in!"

At the front door of the hunting cabin, Ellie turned the key, and after a few tense seconds, the stood in the main room where Bob Stanton knelt in front of a box, back turned to them.

"Hands above your head!" she commanded.

"This is a misunderstanding!"

"I said—"

"Yes, yes." He obliged, much to Ellie's relief. She had come to hate dealing with suspects that only seemed to react to a man's voice. Fortunately, Stanton knew he didn't have a choice. "I just found this myself. I don't know where it came from."

As Ellie put the cuffs on him, Derek glanced into the box.

"Whoa. Is it Christmas or what?"

The box held a hunting knife with rusty red stains. At a closer look, Ellie saw tiny pieces of fabric stick to the blade. Also in the box, a pair of earrings.

"I don't know how this got here. I swear, I didn't kill anyone." He was sweating now.

"Mr. Stanton, I guess you'll have to explain to us about the break-in at your house," Ellie told him.

Christmas indeed, with all the evidence they needed to tie him to the Rena Kelly murder and lean harder on him regarding his deal with Ryan Lemont.

Was this too easy?

Ellie pushed aside the nagging feeling. She had always known Stanton was involved in something bad, and here was the confirmation laid out for them to see. The women who got away, including his ex-wife, were incredibly lucky.

INFATUATIONS

Today wasn't completely horrible after all.

Chapter Nineteen

"Congratulations! This is big."

Back at the station, Ellie indulged herself for a moment, accepting congratulations and a long hug from Jordan.

"I'm so glad you're okay," she whispered.

"Yeah, me too."

"And I guess I'm not going to get out of here anytime soon," Ellie said as she stepped back.

"That's okay. I still have work to do as well. I'll see you later. Derek?"

"Given that this is my case—" Waters cut in.

"Detective Waters, I'd like to talk to you for a moment." Everyone turned around at the lieutenant's voice. "I think everyone, including Detective Henderson, is up to date." No one objected. "Let's get this done," he directed at Ellie and Derek. A somewhat demure Detective Waters followed him into his office, while Ellie and Derek left for the interrogation room where Bob Stanton was waiting. He had lost the cocky attitude a while ago.

"Okay, Mr. Stanton," Ellie said before she sat across from him. "Let's make this as quick and painless as possible for everyone involved. Your dealings with Ryan Lemont, your cousin Harry Travis...You need to tell the whole truth."

"I will, okay? This has gotten way too far."

Behind them, Derek coughed. Talk about an understatement.

"We're listening."

"A huge part of this is your fault. The police are doing nothing, sitting on their hands, someone has to do something, right? It all started with those bums, Raynor, always in everyone's faces for money. They spend it all on drugs and booze anyway."

Ellie thought that the kind of money Raynor might have gotten from begging to tourists would not get him into business with Lemont or any of the small-time drug dealers, but she let Stanton ramble.

"Anyway, Harry approached me and said he might know someone who could help us."

Again, it wasn't very logical trying to "clean up" the neighborhood by getting involved with Lemont, but Bob Stanton had his own version of logic.

"We knew we had to do something. On the one side of the park, it's the beggars, on the other they sell drugs to schoolgirls. Harry said that Ryan Lemont wasn't like that—he only supplied for celebrity parties and such. I mean, who cares what they're doing in their houses?"

"You believed him?"

"Why wouldn't I? He's family. We have the same values."

"So he arranged the meeting that you and Jarrod Tanner attended."

"Jarrod is a good kid."

"Let me guess. Same values," Derek said. Stanton ignored him.

"Ryan said he'd take care of the bums if we did regular raids where the other drug dealers were hanging around. That sounded fair enough."

"You talked to him about Raynor? The one you were especially angry at?"

"I may have mentioned him, yes. We talked about the murders in the park, and how Raynor was trying to make himself look important."

"You told Lemont you wanted him gone?"

"No! Yes...but I didn't say to kill him. I might have made an offhanded comment. Afterwards, Ryan got this idea that I owed him."

"You're saying Lemont murdered Marco Raynor, because he thought you'd asked him to?"

"He doesn't do these things himself, doesn't like to get his hands dirty, but he does give the okay, just like with the waitress."

"Wait, not so fast," Derek interjected. "I'd like to hear more about that misunderstanding. The one with Lemont. We'll get to Rena Kelly and your hunting knife in a moment. Tell us more about that offhanded comment."

"Okay, I said they're like vermin, and this one is especially bad. Lemont said something about rat poison taking care of that, and we laughed it off."

"Laughed it off?" Derek repeated skeptically. "By then, you had to know that he got people killed."

"Yeah, but...anyway. Harry told me it was a bad idea to tell him no, and things were going well. I had no idea. Apparently, the waitress had seen them in the park, and Ryan sent Harry to talk to her. I went with him but waited outside. When I went to find him, he was standing over her. I know what you want to say, but I couldn't talk to the police. Look what happened to Harry."

Ellie noticed that he didn't seem to be scared for his life now. He might still be bending the truth to his advantage. However, she had no trouble believing that Ryan Lemont had orchestrated the murders. "Harry shot Marco Raynor as well? Then who killed him?"

"One of Ryan's goons, I'm sure. He doesn't like loose ends."

"We're going to need names. What about Jarrod or any of the members of your watch? Did you share any of those details with them?"

He shook his head.

"No, I was always the one to negotiate with him. Jarrod knew about the plan to kick out the minor dealers, but that was it. I can give you some names."

For the first time, Ellie actually believed he was telling the whole truth.

"There's just one more thing," she said. "Those items in the box."

"Haven't you figured it out by now? That's Lemont trying to set me up. Harry can't talk, and there'll be my fingertips on the knife. When I saw him with the dead body, I didn't even know he had used it."

"You're not afraid of him now?"

"If you're doing your job correctly, he'll go down, right?"

Ellie thought back to the beginning of the case, the women she'd met, alleging the police didn't care much. She wanted to make a difference, for all of them, and she would. Even if Bob Stanton hadn't committed any of the murders, his prints were all over them, pardon the pun.

But he was right: Ryan Lemont was going down as well.

That's what you get for underestimating Nancy Drew.

Before going to work the next day, Jordan and Ellie had picked up Pauline and Ariel to join them at the bakery that had fortunately agreed to re-schedule—again.

Vanilla, chocolate, white chocolate, coffee crème, strawberry. The choices seemed endless, the situation surreal given what happened yesterday.

"I like strawberry," Ellie said, making Jordan laugh.

"No way. A pink wedding cake, that's a bit too much in your face."

"White, then, to go with the dresses?"

"Sure. White is fine." It was a beautiful day, Jordan thought. With Stanton's arrest and subsequent statement, more dirt on Lemont, the city had gotten a bit safer. More arrests of Lemont's associates had followed.

She felt serene and rested. Ellie was proving herself on the job like Jordan had known she would. By proxy, her own case, the murder of Harry Travis, had been solved as well. Time to indulge for a bit. She was glad they had been able to take Ariel to the appointment as well.

"I think it should go with the color of your dresses," the girl said. "White chocolate butter cream."

"If I may, that's generally a good idea. We can have accents in color, like flowers," the owner of the bakery told them. "How many tiers were you thinking about?"

"At least four?" Ariel said, while Ellie came up with "Three?" at the same time. Jordan's "tiers?" had been only in her head. She wasn't going to have another moment, like with the wedding dress that still needed to be fitted once more, but this was still unreal. In a good way.

"Three max," she finally said. "Who's going to eat all of it?" She was well aware of the source of Ariel's excitement. She had seen many weddings in her time at the cult, but all of them had to do with coercion and fear, serving only the men at the top.

This was her first opportunity to see two people take the step for the right reasons, with all the planning and details that involved.

White chocolate, three tiers, all the right reasons. Jordan caught Ellie's gaze on her, the surge of emotion making her eyes well up.

Every day, she was becoming more aware of the big deal this was, not just another point on the checklist for adulthood.

Ellie was right. Everything they'd been through on the way to this—they deserved every moment of it.

***

As she typed her report later that morning, Ellie felt confident, if not entirely happy. She wished they could have uncovered the connections between Lemont and Stanton before this many people died and more felt threatened by these men. They had finally stopped them.

On a private, completely happy note, the wedding preparations were done. All she needed to do on this end was to wait for the wedding day to arrive. She thought she should probably call Madeline again, and drive by the cemetery after work, see if there were flowers again.

When she picked up a file, a small object fell to the floor. Ellie bent to pick it up, realizing she'd have to do another errand. With a little luck, they could have an earlier dinner tonight. Jordan wasn't at her desk, but she sent her a quick text before she printed out her report.

Chapter Twenty

J ordan and Derek had spent part of the day in court with an older case coming up, the judge fortunately moving things along at a bearable pace.

They drove back to the station together, and Derek laughed when she hid a yawn behind her hand. "Short night?"

"You would know all about it. We were lucky to even get pizza in that place at the time. At least this morning, there was coffee with the tasting."

"So that's it?" he asked. "The last step? You're all ready now?"

"All ready," she confirmed.

"Good. There's not going to be a plan B on the day, like your partner bailing you out."

"I won't need one. Again, I'm really sorry about the drama."

"It's a good decision, you know."

Between the two of them, it was clear he wasn't trying to mansplain Jordan's life to her but simply stating the truth. It was a good decision. One of the best she'd ever made.

"Yes, I know. I can't wait."

"So did you make a decision about your birthmother?"

Jordan made a noncommittal sound. "Okay, your score was almost perfect, but now you blew it. Anyway, I think it's decided. She thinks she's not invited, and I'm not going to tell her otherwise. Distance is a good thing. It works for us."

"Okay."

"Are you and Kate coming to dinner with us, or do you have other plans?"

"I'll ask her, but I think she'll be happy to."

When they arrived at the department, Ellie wasn't at her desk, though she hadn't left for home yet.

"She was going out for an errand," Maria Doss said. "She said she'd come back here to meet you to go to dinner."

"Did she say what errand?"

"To return a key." Maria cast a look at her watch. "She wanted to be here by five, finish up some things before you guys came back." She frowned. "You better check on her."

Jordan did, and naturally, her call went to voicemail. She remembered nearly overreacting at the bar, when Ellie had been following a lead of her own, determined not to let that happen again. She called the number again and this time, left a message. "Hey, Derek and I are back at the station. Where are you? Call me when you get this."

To Derek, she said, "You don't have to wait for me."

"It's fine," he assured her. "Maria!"

Already at the door, she turned around.

"What key was she talking about?" he asked as Jordan sat behind Ellie's desk, absent-mindedly leafing through some of the papers. There was the picture of a cabin, the place where Bob Stanton had been arrested. "The key to Tanner's hunting cabin?"

"She didn't say," Maria said, coming back to join them. Jordan didn't like the concern in her tone. "Why? He didn't actually know anything, right? Both Lemont and Stanton said he wasn't involved in anything but that one meeting, where allegedly no murders were discussed?"

"Where's Waters?" Jordan asked, uneasy with the turn of events.

"He went home, but Ellie let him know first. He gets cranky whenever someone else takes initiative."

"Well, he should have gone with her. This is Tanner's number. I'll ask him if she came by." Derek was on the phone a moment later. Jordan heard the signal: This number was out of service.

"Something's not right," she said. "I know a lot of people were arrested, but what if some of Lemont's minions are still out there, taking care of loose ends? That could include Tanner. They won't care that he didn't know anything."

She could read in Derek and Maria's faces that they understood what she wasn't saying. Even if Lemont didn't target her specifically, Ellie could be in the wrong place at the wrong time—and Lemont did have a nickname for her.

"Let's find him," Derek said. "And Ellie, too, so we can finally go for dinner."

His attempt at levity fell flat.

❧

Jarrod Tanner hadn't been in his dorm room, the roommate informing Ellie that he was still at training. When she arrived at the gym though, she saw a group of young men in jerseys leave. Tanner wasn't with them.

"Excuse me. Do you know where I can find Jarrod Tanner? He was supposed to be at training?"

The teen wasn't in a hurry, giving her the once over, his demeanor irritating her. "Do you know—or not? It's important." Madeline. The cemetery. Some work to catch on. She didn't have time for this.

"Yeah, sure. He said he wanted to practice a little while longer. Is he waiting for you?"

Again, with that look. "I don't think so. Thanks."

She passed him by and went inside, walking along the empty hallway, and entered the gym through the girls' locker room.

Walking inside, Ellie stopped cold at the sight: Jarrod Tanner shaking hands with a man who looked familiar. He left through another door in the back, and then it was just her and Jarrod, who came walking towards her quickly.

"Detective. What are you doing here?"

The real question was, what was Lemont's lawyer doing here, talking to the man who had led them to Stanton and the box with the bloody knife? Who was he siding with? The questions multiplied in Ellie's mind, but just as quickly, a possible theory came together.

"You're shopping for a lawyer? I can tell you this one is quite expensive."

"I asked you first." He gave her a crooked smile.

"You were so kind to give us the key to the hunting cabin. Our colleagues will let you know when you can go back, but meanwhile, I thought I'd bring you the key. How are you doing, Jarrod?"

"Me? I'm fine. I'm not the one who hid a bloody knife from the police."

There you have it. Ellie didn't think the knife, or the blood on it, had been mentioned anywhere outside of police reports. "That must be pretty bad for you. We've been told you looked up to Bob."

"Who told you? I mean, of course he was dedicated," he corrected himself quickly. "You gotta appreciate that in a man, right?"

"Right." It was probably wise to leave it at that. "Unfortunately, he's not just that, right? Did you know about that box?"

"No, why would I?"

"Because we both know who put it there, don't we?"

When Tanner reached into his duffel bag, she pulled her gun.

"Don't even try. Turn around. Slowly."

He half-obeyed but looked over his shoulder. "You're making a mistake, Detective Harding. I know my rights, and yes, I have indeed a lawyer, and I can afford him if that's what you—"

"Hands above your head."

Ellie reached for her cell phone with her left hand, cursing herself for not bringing her cuffs while she was still on the job.

That's when he spun around and slammed into her, bringing them both to the floor.

The back door leading to the gym was locked, no sound to be heard from the inside, no one reacting to demands they should come outside with their hands visible. Jordan waited for the sign, then stepped forward and kicked the door open, she and Derek hastening inside the gym.

The court was empty, but in the bleachers, Jordan saw Ellie standing above Jarrod Tanner. He was groaning, holding his bloody nose.

"Bitch punched me," he said as if he couldn't believe it. "I'm going to sue her! In fact, I want to file a report right now."

"I don't think you will," Ellie said behind him. "I recorded everything you told me earlier." She had obviously emerged as the winner, but her reddened knuckles looked painful, and she was pressing a hand against her ribs. "Whoa. You guys are the backup I called for? I'm really glad you're here. I think I need to sit down."

After a trip to the hospital to make sure nothing was broken—nothing was—Ellie wanted dinner after all, insisting that she'd be too wired to get some rest right away. Jordan took it upon herself to make all the remaining decisions for the day.

"Come on, it was only Tylenol. I can have a beer! Hey, do you know how many bad guys I arrested in the past two days?"

"Yeah, that's really great. You can have a sip of mine."

Jordan wasn't going to argue after listening to the recording. Ellie had been on the right track all along, uncovering the cooperation between Stanton and Lemont—what they had all underestimated was Tanner's involvement. He might have started out admiring Stanton, but he had soon found a new hero in the even more ruthless drug dealer. Not that it got him anywhere, at least not at first.

"They treated me like a child," he whined. "No one ever took me seriously."

"Well, I am taking you seriously," Ellie had told him on the tape.

"I realized that Bob was only using me because I had my grandparents' cabin. I even had to come up with the plan to deal in school, or Ryan wouldn't have noticed me. He noticed me all right after I offed the bitch."

"Wait. You're talking about..."

"Rena, the slut. She said she wanted to be with me, while she slept with every guy who came through that backdoor—I found out that she and Ryan were laughing about me."

Jordan remembered those words with a chill. In his quest to be taken seriously, Tanner had become a killer himself. Yes, Waters should have gone with Ellie, if only to follow protocol. She hoped there'd be consequences.

Ellie had been lucky. They all had been, only because she'd been able to overpower him. There had been a gun in that duffel bag. Lemont's lawyer turned out to be the last witness to help them put the pieces together.

She handed her beer over to Ellie who drank a bit more from it than she should have.

"Don't look at me like that. I'm going to eat, all right?"

She ordered a burger with fries, and she wasn't as generous with her fries as Jordan had been with her beer. *Just as well*, she thought, her mind a mix of exhaustion and gratitude. *I'll have to fit into that dress.*

Chapter Twenty-One

J ordan and Ellie had both refused Kate's suggestion that they'd spend the night before the wedding in different quarters, but in the morning, Jordan had stolen away to Jack and Pauline's to get ready for the day. Pauline's eyes started welling up the moment she opened the door to Jordan, and she kept a pack of tissues with her.

"Smile. It's a happy occasion," Jordan reminded her, even though she couldn't recall the last time she'd been this nervous. This was uncharted territory, and everyone's eyes would be on her in less than two hours. Well, not everyone's, but those that mattered.

"Oh yes. It's right up there when we knew we could bring you home…Oh honey. I'm sorry."

"Don't be," Jordan assured her. "Just don't say things like that after the make-up is on."

Make-up, too, and a photographer because this was a once-in-a-lifetime event. She remembered Derek's comment about Jim and Kathryn as well as Jack and Pauline being successful in their marriages in their own way. Nurture, nature, apparently, she had it all on her side.

Most importantly, she had Ellie. Together, they would navigate whatever the road ahead held for them.

Ellie wondered for a moment if they had really invited all these people, then she took a deep breath and willed herself to relax. Her best friend was by her side, Derek, and Jordan's parents were with her somewhere close by.

As she caught Kate's gaze on her, Ellie couldn't help thinking back to the hardship her friend had to face not long ago, the grief she had to overcome. There was an understanding between them. Ellie grieved, too, for two people who couldn't be here on this most important day of all.

"This is your day," Kate said. "It's okay to think of only you for now."

"Thank you."

"Thank you. I'm happy to be here for you. Ready?"

"I was born ready." Ellie laughed, though her vision momentary blurred. She couldn't have that. She still had to make it all the way to the officiant's desk, and through the vows. She didn't want to rush through any of it either but enjoy every second of it.

"All right then. You have your flowers. Old, new, borrowed, blue?"

"You double and triple checked with me earlier. Yes, I have everything."

She was wearing a bracelet that had belonged to Meredith Harding, given to her by her mother, Ellie's grandmother, a long time ago. Her earrings were borrowed from Kate, and Pauline had paid for the brand-new shoes that would put her on eye-level with her bride. Regarding something blue, Kate had to take her word for it, because this item was for Jordan's eyes only.

Everything was arranged so that the first look would truly be a surprise for both of them. Jordan had only mentioned that the latest fitting had been successful. Their friends and family who had come shopping with them would make sure that style and color didn't clash. The music started, and Ellie felt herself trembling. Of all the achievements in her life, she considered this one of the biggest. She knew that Jordan would go first, with her parents, Derek as the best man, Kate, and finally Ellie. Even though they had discussed it beforehand, Ellie felt a pang of regret, and even the small stretch from the hallway through the aisle to the desk seemed incredibly long.

"Ellie. It's time."

Pauline, appearing out of nowhere, startled her.

"Slight change of plans, if you're all right with it. We thought Jack and Jordan would go first, and I'd walk you down the aisle? We should welcome you into the family properly." When Ellie was unable to react right away, she said, "I know, sweetie. We can't replace your parents, and I know you wish they could be here now, but we'll be here for you. We're so happy Jordan found you."

Kate gave her a gentle push, and Ellie finally found the words.

"Thank you so much. I am happy too—and this is perfect."

"That's settled then. Let's go."

Ellie had been afraid that she wouldn't be able to get out a word, let alone vows, but when she stepped into the room, her attention wasn't on any of the smiling guests. Pauline gently steered her forward. Ellie forgot about everyone but Jordan, and the promise they were going to make. And there was no way she could hurry anything in those heels. Finally, she had made it all the way, and they took each other's hands.

"You look amazing," she whispered, already anticipating that all of the pictures would show her staring in awe.

Jordan smiled, self-conscious, as if she wanted to argue. Instead, she just whispered back, "Thank you. How many inches?"

Ellie held her gaze, amused. "Just enough so I could make it from the car, and back. Your mom bought them for me. She has faith in me."

"I have every faith in you. In us."

Just like that, the conversation wasn't about shoes any longer, and Ellie didn't think it was necessary to mention that she'd be wearing a different pair for the reception.

The music stopped, and the officiant began the ceremony.

Ellie held on tighter, and she found that when it was her turn, she said all the right words at the right time, including the most important ones.

"I do."

She would never forget that moment.

❧

For the most part of the day, Jordan would hold on to Ellie with one hand, and to a champagne glass with the other, or so it seemed. She couldn't let go of her. She couldn't stop smiling, and eventually, she managed to relax, the stress of many months, for many reasons, falling away. The champagne might have played a role in that as well, but it wasn't the main reason.

She'd never imagined this would feel so much like a major piece of her life falling into place, a game changer. Most of the people in the room with them had been confronted with some of the worst of humanity, still, they kept believing in something good, had put aside all their own issues and problems to be here with her and Ellie today.

Ellie—she had finally been able to let go for a second—stood with Becca Crane and Ariel, both of them looking happy and excited. Pauline was talking to Madeline, Ellie's mother's friend. Darla held her toddler on her knees, and in another corner, Derek and Kate were having a quiet immersed conversation. She could have sworn he had shed a tear or two during the ceremony. Not that Jordan could blame him.

She walked over to Ellie and their guests—apparently there was only so long she could bear to be apart in a crowded room. "Could I borrow my wife for a moment?"

She noticed Ellie's face light up at Jordan's use of the term. "I think people are going to want to dance, so we should give them a good example."

She knew Ellie had been a tad worried about this part, because they hadn't had time to practice much, but it was for exactly that reason that they'd chosen a slow song. As soon as Ellie was in her arms, Jordan knew they weren't going to embarrass themselves.

"Do you think we could steal away for a bit after this?"

"Already?" Ellie gave her a knowing smile. "Everyone will know...not that I'm not interested, I definitely am. But once I get out of this dress, I don't think I can put it on again—"

"It's not that," Jordan confessed. "I mean, of course it's that, and I want to, but...I'm so hungry. I couldn't eat much earlier, and every other minute someone put a glass in front of me."

"Oh God, I know what you mean." Ellie laughed. "It's an amazing day, but it's our day. Come on. I don't care what they think, let's get some of that cake, and maybe someone will make us a coffee."

"I love you," Jordan said, and even though it might be self-evident on a day like this, at this moment, she blushed, feeling utterly naked.

"I love you too," Ellie said, leaning in to kiss her. "Forever. It's official now."

She put the last piece on her wall, another important piece of the puzzle. She had to know all of them inside out, anticipate what they'd think, say, or do in every situation. And she was damn good at it too, so good that no one had suspected her so far. Five years, and she was just getting started.

First contact was only a few days away, and already she had perfectly adopted her new life. She had studied the people and relationships that came with it. A much bigger challenge than the others, that much was for sure. There'd be a barrage of questions, suspicion, but she was well-prepared as usual.

She reached out to trace a finger over the photograph.

"Such an amazing coincidence," she whispered. "I'm so happy I found you."

On her way out of the apartment, she stopped at the mirror in the hallway, smiling at her reflection, practicing the perfect expression for what she was about to say:

"Hi. My name is Natalie. I'm your sister."

About the Author

B arbara Winkes writes sapphic crime drama and Christmas romance. She loves writing characters who get the
job done, whether it's stopping a predator or saving cherished
traditions—while still making time for love. She lives with her
wife in Quebec City.

barbarawinkes.com

Also by Barbara Winkes

The Crossing Lines Trilogy
Undercover
Redemption
Vengeance

The Connected Series
Promised to the Queen
Drawn to the Enemy
Tempted by the Protector

Kelli & Merin Romantic Suspense
Thunder
Rain

Standalone
The Amnesia Project